When Mr Fullerman told us in class that we could spend our (**GOLDEN TIME***) finishing off work or reading, I made this

VERY IMPORTANT LIST:

THINGS I WANT TO DO THIS WEEKEND ☺

1. Eat a BIG breakfast.  mmmm

2. Draw a NEW **DOGZOMBIES** T-shirt

   (with Derek).

3. FIND a SUPER HERO costume for Leroy's party.

4. Make a birthday card.

5. Watch some GOOD TV shows.

6. Try a new flavour of crisps.

   (Always good to do something NEW.)

*Golden time – when we're allowed to do anything we want.

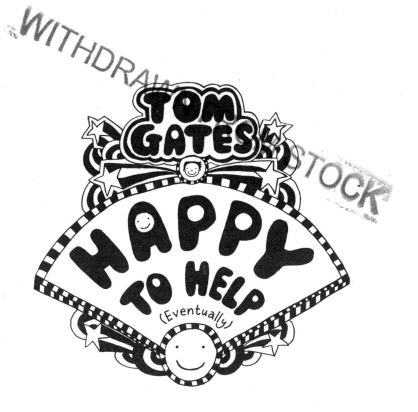

TOM GATES

HAPPY TO HELP
(Eventually)

By LiZ PiCHON

(who is KEEN for you to read this book)

SCHOLASTIC

AMY looked over my shoulder and said,

Marcus didn't agree (OBVIOUSLY).

"Why are you even MAKING
        a list?" he asked.

Nice list.

Thanks!

 "So I don't forget what I want to do."
   Then Marcus pointed to my number 4.

"I've made a card with my AMAZING brand new
        PENS already."

 That's good... I told him.

"I've got LOADS of pens in all different
colours, so I drew a card for Leroy.
I'm good at drawing."

  Yes, you are, Marcus.

Then he pointed at number 3 on my list.

"I've done that one too – MY costume is the BEST."

"Of course it is, Marcus." I rolled my eyes because everything Marcus does is the BEST (according to him).

"Hey, Tom, can you guess what I'm going to the party as?" he asked. "Go on – have a guess ... go on ... go on... Can you guess? Bet you can't."

 I wasn't in the mood for guessing games, so I made something up. "Errrmm, you're going as

SUPER GRUMPY HERO."

Huh?

"That's not a REAL superhero," Marcus told me.

 "Are you kidding? Everyone knows about SUPER GRUMPY HERO."

"No they don't! You're just trying to be FUNNY."

"Choosing the right costume is a serious business, Marcus – unless you're a clown," I told him, which made AMY LAUGH out loud.

Marcus didn't LAUGH.

"You'll just have to wait now. I'm not telling you what my costume is," he replied – a little bit smugly.

 "OK," I said as I really wasn't that bothered. THIS made Marcus even MORE desperate to tell me.

"I COULD let you know because it's amazing, but ... I don't feel like it now." He smirked.

 Fine - no need to tell me. I'll live.

"It's SUCH a good **SUPERHERO** costume," Marcus muttered, still not giving up.

AMY got bored of listening to our endless chat about costumes and said,

 MARCUS IS GOING AS SUPERHERO CAT BOY, aren't you, Marcus?

"**AMY**! You spoilt my Surprise and how did you EVEN KNOW?"

Marcus asked in a slightly CROSS way.

 "Errrrr, because you told me - you've been going on about it for weeks," **AMY** reminded him.

"That's because it's the **BEST** costume ever,"

Marcus said (AGAIN).

 "Not as good as a **SUPER GRUMPY HERO** costume,"

I said and NUDGED him, but Marcus still didn't LAUGH.

I decided to add TWO more things to my list:

7. Don't dress up as **SUPERHERO** CAT Boy for the party (like Marcus).

8. Spend **MORE** time RELAXING. Because that's what weekends are for.

I wake up and open my eyes and the FIRST thing I see is the LIST I stuck to my wall.

I look at number 1.

Eat a BIG breakfast.

EXCELLENT, I can do that right now.

BUT there could be a problem.

COMIC

I can HEAR Mum and Dad STOMPING up and down the stairs right outside

my room.

It sounds like they're VERY busy moving things around and putting stuff away, which can only mean one thing.

It's a "TIDY UP SATURDAY."

Oh no.

Normally, I'd keep out of their way or look very BUSY so Mum and Dad wouldn't give me any BORING jobs to do.

(It's happened before.)

"TOM! Can you take these UPSTAIRS?"

Oh...

"TOM! Can you take these downstairs?"

Oh...

Tom, here are some nail scissors to cut the edge of the grass. See you in ten hours.

Tom, can you put away the dishes?

BYE.

I don't mind helping, but it's ALWAYS at the wrong time. Like right NOW when I want to ✓ tick number 1 off my list and ...

MAKE A BIG BREAKFAST.

Delia is a WORLD CLASS EXPERT at not helping out. Whenever Mum and Dad are doing a tidy up, I've noticed she says things like:

Sure – no problem. I'll be down soon...

(Then never appears.)

⬇

OK – I'm just taking a shower.

(And stays there for ever.)

I would take out the bins – but I'm in my pyjamas.

⬇

Like THAT'S an excuse? Although I might keep my pyjamas on today just in case.

Peeking around my bedroom door, it LOOKS like Mum and Dad are downstairs. The radio is on and I can HEAR Dad ♪ singing while he cleans. I say "SINGING", but it's more of a weird WARBLE. Mum thinks he sounds like a SEAL with toothache.

(I agree – if that's what a seal with toothache sounds like.)

As I'm on my way to the kitchen, I can see Dad through the crack in the door vacuuming like crazy. Mum's plumping up cushions on the sofa in a very aggressive way. She's giving them a BIG karate CHOP, which is alarming.

Boff
Boff
Boff
Boff

MUM – 10
CUSHIONS – 1

While they're busy, this is the PERFECT time to make myself a BIG breakfast. Yum!

The kitchen is already looking all clean and spotless, thanks to Mum and Dad's morning tidy up.

I start by SEARCHING for cereal and checking all the cupboards. I'm SURE Delia has hidden the GOOD cereal. So I keep looking until

I STRIKE

CEREAL GOLD

YES!

CRUNCHY MUNCHIES

There's a BRAND NEW, unopened BOX of **CRUNCHY MUNCHIES** just waiting to be eaten (by me).

I grab a BIGGER bowl than I'm normally allowed and try to open up the cereal packet by holding it under my arm and RIPPING the top off...

RrRiPPPPPPP

At exactly the same time

as the BOTTOM FALLS

OPEN.

Cereal pours out all over the floor.

"Awww no, how did that happen?"

(Opening it upside down didn't help.)

I try scooping UP the cereal with my hands, PLONK some in my bowl and then scrape as much as I can back into the box. The FLOOR'S clean (thanks to Mum and Dad). There are no bits of FLUFF or anything grim – that I can see, anyway.

With the cereal under control, I help myself to milk, then orange juice, which is tricky to pour. The juice doesn't want to go into my glass.

It's trickling over my hand on to the table

and DRIP

DRIP

DRIP

DRIPPING on to the floor as well.

"Awwww, what?"

I spot a couple of nice-looking clean tea towels that do the trick wiping up the spills.

I've done more cleaning than eating so far and this needs to change FAST!

There's a loaf of knobbly brown bread that's covered in bits, so I leave that and grab the LAST two slices of white bread. Perfect for toast doodles. PRESSING my finger down HARD into the soft white bread, I write TOM on one and draw a smiley face on the other. Then I put both slices into the toaster and wait. A sneaky custard cream keeps me going while I enjoy the SMELL of the bread toasting.

Unless it burns.

I'm careful NOT to let this happen.

15

In the cupboard there are ROWS and ROWS of "special jam" that Granny Mavis makes. No one knows what's in it, but Granny keeps bringing us MORE because she thinks we LIKE it. I think it looks

 SUSPICIOUS and choose the squeezy **HONEY.**

The TOAST P O P S up looking FANTASTIC!

I can still see my name nice and clear even after I've covered both slices with butter and **HONEY.**

I'm FINALLY enjoying my handiwork when Delia walks into the kitchen in her pyjamas, clutching a bottle of water.

Morning!

I say in a nice cheery way.
Delia makes NO eye ⊗⊗ contact.

Grump----->

Then her feet slip and she DRAMATICALLY

S L I D E S

across the floor in a very
IMPRESSIVE way.

Whoooooo whoooo ahhhhh whooo

Uh-oh...

WhOoooOa

Delia grips her water bottle SO TIGHTLY a jet of water SHOOTS UP and SOAKS her in the face. Because I'm a nice brother, I pass her a tea towel first and then say...

Joke

Hey, Delia – how was your trip?

"Very funny, Tom," Delia says while wiping her face.

"WHAT'S THAT ON THE FLOOR?"

"It's the water you just spilt,"

 I say, pointing out the obvious.

Now she's got bits of orange from the juice

← Bits of orange

on her face. (I keep quiet.)

"What HAVE you been doing, Tom?

There's cereal all over the place."

"Is there?"

I say like it's a **SHOCK**.

"Have you taken the last two slices of bread?"

she adds, peering into the almost

empty bread bin.

"No, I've left that brown *knobbly bread* BREAD stuff."

Delia GLARES at it.

"I'm not eating that – it's stale."

"Here – have this bit if you want?"
I offer her a slightly nibbled bit of my
toast that says "OM" on it.

"No, thanks – I like my toast without my little
brother's fingers stuck in it."

Suit yourself!

At least I offered.

Grrr Rrrr Grrr Rhrrrr

The "NOISE" of a vacuum cleaner going across the
ceiling interrupts our chat.

21

"Mum and Dad are doing a BIG SATURDAY TIDY UP," I tell Delia.

"I guessed."

"Do you think they'll ask us to do lots of jobs round the house?"

"Probably, but I'm busy," Delia says.

"Busy doing what?"

Bye

 I ask her, but Delia's already LEFT.

This feels like a good time to eat what's left of my HONEY toast, so I put it on a plate and head to the front room.

Thanks to Mum's EXTRA strong arms, the sofa and cushions are nicely "PLUMPED" up and SQUISHY. The rug feels all FLUFFY under my feet too. I do a great BIG...

22

LEAP, my TOAST flies OFF the plate, then lands on the rug

... **honey** side down.

CLOSE-UP OF MY TOAST

"Awwww, I wanted to eat that."

The toast's now got bits of RUG on

it and there's a sticky mess on the floor.

I nip to the kitchen to find a TEA TOWEL (again)

so I can wipe it up.

Delia's reappeared to have her breakfast.

She's eating a bowl of MY **CRUNCHY MUNCHIES**

and sighs when she sees me.

"What have you done NOW, Tom?"

"Nothing..." I say.

"Have you dropped your toast on the floor?"

"No."

"If it's been on the floor, don't eat it," Delia tells me while she's eating cereal that's been on the floor.

(I keep THAT quiet - OBVIOUSLY.)

I take the tea towel and try to give the rug a wipe. But I think I've made it worse.

The 😐 **BEST** thing I can do now is ...

... *MOVE* the small table over ➡ the **STAIN** so no one can see it.

There: all done.

Sitting back down, I turn on the TV and I'm just about to start watching it when Mum comes in looking a bit **SURPRISED**.

What's happened in the kitchen, Tom?

 "I made my own breakfast," I say proudly.

"It was tidy this morning. Now it looks like we've been burgled!"

 "Delia IS very messy," I point out.

Mum's staring at the table I moved,

so I tell her about Leroy's party as

a DISTRACTION.

"HEY, Mum! I need to get a present for Leroy's birthday."

Mum moves the table back to where it was, and I hold my breath.

"I don't have time today. Maybe Delia can help. I'll ask her," Mum says and leaves the room without noticing the **STAIN.**

PHEW!

I move the table back over the stain and carry on watching TV.

It's an EXCELLENT NEW episode of the Jolly Fruit Bunch – another thing TICKED ✓ OFF my list.

I'm just getting to a GOOD bit when Delia suddenly appears and ...

... TuRNs IT OFF!

"HEY!"

"Get dressed – thanks to you we're going out." CLICK

"We are? Where?"

"The shops – anywhere we can get this present you told Mum you need,"

Delia snaps.

Then Dad suddenly pops his head round the door.

"There you both are! It's TIDY uP SATuRDAY! I can tell by your cheery faces that you're KEEN to help out! I need a hand with the windows and someone to hold the ladder."

"I would, but I'm helping Mum already. I'm taking Tom to get a present for his friend," Delia says.

"You're both still in your pyjamas," Dad points out, but Delia has already LEFT THE ROOM.

Gone

(Once again AVOIDING doing ANY JOBS.)

"I'm going with Delia..." I tell Dad, then I follow Delia upstairs and get dressed so I can keep up with her. She's EVEN got to the bathroom before me (OF COURSE she has).

Annoying.

Knock knock tap

I wait outside and knock on the door to let her know I'm waiting.

(I know this annoys her so she'll be quicker.) My knuckles are just starting to get tired when she comes out.

"You're lucky I haven't changed my mind about taking you out. Hurry up."

"**I**'ll be QUICK!" I say, then help myself to the nice, clean towels in the super sparkly bathroom (all thanks to Mum and Dad – again).
Brushing my teeth and **GArgling** with water while singing "Delia's a Weirdo" isn't easy.

But I keep going...

When I go downstairs, Delia says, You took your time.

I don't tell her what I was doing.

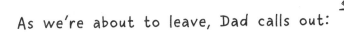She's waiting for me with her arms folded and looking irritated already.

"I'm here now," I say with a smile.

As we're about to leave, Dad calls out:

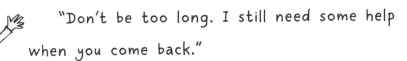"Don't be too long. I still need some help when you come back."

OK, Dad, we won't!

I call back and by the time I turn around, Delia is already halfway down the road.

Huh...

I have to RUN to catch up with her.

Hey! Wait for me!

"Listen to me, Tom, we're not going far –
        just to the local shops,"
            Delia tells me.

    "Why not the shopping centre?"
I ask, as that's much better for presents.

    "It's too busy – and I don't want you looking
            at EVERYTHING and taking too long."

"BUT I'll need to look around. I have to get
something Leroy actually likes."
(Leroy's party isn't for AGES, but I'm not saying
that NOW.)

Delia SIGHS heavily.
    "What does he like then?"

The same
things as me!

I think for a minute, then give her a

BIG list:

 books,  pens,  games, toys, card games, nice chocolate, treats,  T -shirts, dogs, movies, cheese puffs

and MAGIC TRICKS.

"Just pick **ONE** thing, and we'll get that."

"Where are we going?"

I ask.

"That **ODD** household shop, the one that sells everything," Delia tells me. "It's on that parade of shops round the corner."

"An **ODD** shop? Can't we go to a nice shop?"

"Hurry up, Tom."

I have to run to catch up with her again.

Delia stops outside a shop which has **ALL** kinds of household STUFF hanging up on the walls around the front of the building. There are brooms, pots of paint, plates, bags , umbrellas, funny figures you put in the garden – so many **ODD** things.

In here, she says.

Really?

I pull a face at the **ODD** shop as it doesn't look like a good shop for a present for Leroy ...

... until we go inside!

There's an ENTIRE WALL filled with toys, trick jokes, games and lots of drawing stuff too.

"Find something for your friend and don't get DISTRACTED," Delia tells me.

I'm already looking at a GIANT rubber snake that's got Leroy's name all over it.

"NO - not that," Delia groans.

"Why not? It's perfect!"
I lunge towards her, holding the head of the rubber snake.

"Because it's horrible and far too BIG."

"EXACTLY, that's the whole point."
I can't believe I have to explain that.

"Find something else."

Reluctantly, I put the snake back (for now). Walking round the shop, I study everything on the shelves carefully. WHY didn't I know about this place before?

There's something for EVERY occasion. Fake ICE CUBES with spiders in. (Good choice!) Or a stick-on EYE for your forehead; even several sets of wind-up false teeth that walk around.

After a LOT of careful thinking, I choose two very realistic trick fried eggs and a pack of MAGIC cards. Leroy will love them!

AMAZINGLY, Delia pays for everything and also buys some paints for herself.

We're both happy with our stuff and in a good mood.

"Let's go," Delia tells me.

Jolly

But I SPOT something that makes my EYES open even **wider.**

"Look, Delia! LOOK at that

ART BOX.

Isn't it AMAZING?"

I tell her.

She doesn't seem that interested. I open it up to have a closer look: this **ART BOX** has got

EVERYTHING I'VE EVER WANTED

AND MORE!

Inside there are pens, /pencils, 🥫paints, ⬜rubbers, felt tip pens, soft crayons and all kinds of art stuff. Every drawer I open reveals something amazing! I could use this to make my new **DOGZOMBIES** T-shirts, and so many other things too.

THIS IS EXCITING!

Delia puts her hand on my shoulder and tries to turn me around to leave.

"This way, Tom..."

"But what about the **ART BOX?**"

I say LOUDLY.

"We've already got a present."

"NO – not for Leroy, for ME!"
I sigh and stare at it some more, then run my hands over the pencils that form a neat rainbow.

"Forget it, Tom. It's too expensive and it's not even your birthday."

"I'll buy it myself then with my OWN pocket money. I've got a money box at home and some change here." piggy ← bank

I have a rummage in my pocket and bring out ... a wafer wrapper.

"That's not going to buy you much, Tom,"

Delia tells me.

Oh...

I'm still staring at the **ART BOX** when a little girl comes over and calls out:

"Hey, Dad, LOOK at this ART BOX!"

My hand is still holding the handle like it's mine.

Her dad comes over and she LOOKS at him with BIG PLEADING EYES and says,

"Can we get it, Dad? Pleeease?"

Huh?

"It does look like it's got EVERYTHING you need," her dad tells her.

I'm thinking, It's got EVERYTHING I NEED TOO!

I TURN to Delia and try out the same PLEADING EYES.

 "Come on then. Let's go and buy it. It can be an early birthday present," the dad says and for a moment I think he's talking to me ⇨ and get EXCITED.

YES!

Only he's not.

It gets awkward when I try and pick up the **ART BOX** at the same time the little girl does.

 "LET GO of the **ART BOX**,"
Delia tells me.

Reluctantly, I do.

"It was the last one..." I whisper sadly as the little girl and her dad take the **ART BOX** to the counter to pay for it.

I sigh LOUDLY. "Gone for ever."

 "It's NOT the last one, Tom. I can see there's another one on the shelves,"
Delia tells me.

I'm HOPING this means she is about to become the best sister in the whole wide world 🌍 and

BUY IT FOR ME? ☺

"**Bad** luck, Tom – you can't have everything you want. That's life. Now let's go."

"But I don't want EVERYTHING – I just want **THAT ART BOX**,"

I tell her. But Delia's had enough of my pleading eyes and has already left the shop.   Oh.

All the way home I keep thinking about HOW I can get myself one of those **ART BOXES.**

"You're quiet for a change," Delia says.

"I'm making PLANS and thinking."

"That sounds dangerous..."
she whispers.

Plans...

"Very funny."

Look, Tom – Mum and Dad don't have the money to spend on **ART BOXES** right now. You might have to wait.

"I'm going to try and buy it myself. I'll do every job I can and earn more pocket money."

Delia LAUGHS. "That's going to take a LONG time. You'll be as OLD as Mum and Dad by the time you've earnt enough money."

 "Really? THAT OLD?"

"Yes. How about you get a smaller **ART BOX?**" Delia asks me.

"It won't be the same."

"That's right. It'll be smaller – but that's better than nothing."

I don't answer.

When I get home, I look at my list and ADD in BIG LETTERS:

EARN EXTRA MONEY to BUY the ART BOX OF MY DREAMS.

Then I check inside my money box to see how much I already have. I turn it upside down and give it a GOOD "SHAKE."

Out comes ...

an old sweet ...

a few coins ...

a paper clip ...

... and the key to my diary.

I've been looking for that!

Oh... Saving enough money for the **ART BOX** of my dreams might take longer than I thought. (I'm happy to find the key to my diary, though.*) I will offer to help ALL THE TIME – EVERY DAY – for however long it takes.

STARTING WITH

RIGHT NOW

as it __is__ Tidy Up Saturday ☺ after all.

*Now I can open it and read all my old secrets!

Mum is busy sweeping up the bits of cereal
I dropped earlier. This is the PERFECT
time for me to step in and offer to help.

"Hi, Mum – I can do that OR any other
jobs you need help with," I say enthusiastically.

"You're too late, Tom. I've done it now.
You could have helped out more this morning.
What's brought this on?"

"Pocket money!" I say a bit too quickly, so I
add: "AND I really want to BE HELPFUL."

"OK – you want to do jobs for pocket money?"
Mum repeats.

"YES, I'll do ANYTHING."

"ANYTHING? I'd better make the most of this.
You can hang out the washing – that's a good
start," Mum suggests.

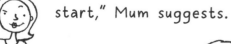

(This is an EASY JOB.)

"I can do THAT!" I smile and look

SUPER KEEN.

 "Great! AND how about you clean up that STAIN you left on the carpet and tried to hide with the table as well?"

Oh...

I pretend to look SURPRISED like it's NEWS to me.

"What was the STAIN?" she wants to know.

"It's a MYSTERY," I say as convincingly as I can. Mum hands me some gloves, cleaning spray and a cloth, so I add,

I'M ALWAYS HAPPY TO HELP ☺

(eventually).

 **M**um watches as I keep spraying, then I give it a good wipe.

Getting there, Tom. Keep going,

she tells me.

It takes me a few goes, but eventually the **STAIN** comes out.

 "This cleaning stuff is **VERY** tiring."

"Ready for the next job then, Tom?" Mum asks me.

"Oh yes, I can't wait. I'm so **READY**," I say. I might even offer to help Delia, then she will see I'm SERIOUS about buying the **ART BOX** myself.

Mum brings a basket of washing down.

"I'll put the washing powder in. Remember what happened last time YOU did it, Tom?"*

*In *Spectacular School Trip (Really)* I added too much powder.

"Hmmm, sort of. I can do the rest of the washing, though," I say with a confident SMILE.

Mum talks me through what to do.

"Put the washing in, close the door and **PRESS** that button.

When it's finished, the LIGHT  flashes and you can OPEN the door and hang all the washing outside to dry.

Got that, Tom?"

Mum gives me very CLEAR instructions, but the moment she goes back to work

I forget.

The machine looks half empty to me.
I'm SURE I could fit some more stuff in
there, like the tea towels for a start.
I do a quick run around the house and grab
any clothes I think could do with a wash.
My socks, a few things from
school, then I SPOT a BIG pile of
Delia's clothes that she's left on her bedroom floor.

Imagine how happy she'd be if I did all
her washing for her?

Thank you, Tom, you're the
BEST little brother EVER.

That's ME!

I can SEE it now.

Have some pocket money, Tom, OK?

I'm thinking about Delia being nice to me for a change. I take all the extra clothes and SHOVE them in the machine, which is VERY FULL. Then I shut the door and TURN THE DIAL TO SUPER FAST TURBO EXTRA HOT.

SUPERFAST TURBO EXTRA HOT

This washing will be done in

NO TIME AT ALL. ☺

Once that's all done, I go and find Dad to see if HE'S got any jobs for me to do.

So far, today is going really well.

ART BOX

I find Dad in his shed.

"I'm ready to **HELP OUT** if you've got any jobs for me to do?" I ask him.

"We could have done with your help this morning," Dad reminds me. "How tidy is your room?"

"VERY TIDY. It's PERFECT," I say.

(It's NOT.)

Bedroom tidying doesn't count as an extra pocket money job. As we're chatting, a **WASP** starts **BUZZING** around our heads, which is VERY annoying.

Dad SHOOOOS it out of the window, which gives him an idea.

"How good are you at washing windows, Tom?"

I'm the BEST window cleaner ever.

"Great! You can clean the OUTSIDE of these windows and I'll do the inside," Dad tells me.

They'll be the cleanest windows you've ever seen, Dad.

For extra pocket money,

I add happily.

Now I have TWO jobs on the go, I can almost IMAGINE the **ART BOX** of my dreams getting closer.

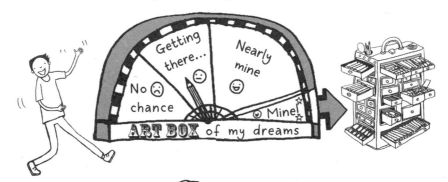

HAPPY TO HELP clean windows

"I'm all SET," I tell Dad.

Big yellow sponge

Tiny sponge

Squeegee

Bucket of water

I've got everything I need to get cleaning.

"You know what to do?"

I nod.

Dad goes into the house to make some phone calls

and leaves me to wash the shed windows.

THIS IS GOING TO BE THE EASIEST JOB EVER!

I start at the top of the window and use both sponges at once.

My arms are already starting to ache from all the MOVING around. It's not making the windows very clean. I'm just **SMEARING** all the dirt around. What I need is more **SOAPY** water. Washing-up liquid from the kitchen will do the trick.

I add a good SQUEEEEZEEE into my bucket.

Then I run back to turn the water on and it shoots into the bucket. Straight away loads of bubbles appear.

The bubbles keep getting ...

BIGGER AND BIGGER

Then they start
spilling over
the side of
the bucket.

This is EXACTLY what I wanted: lots of bubbly,
soapy water.

Every time I PLUNGE the two sponges into the bucket and **SQUEEZE** them, I make MORE and MORE bubbles.

I manage to cover the whole side of the shed with FOAMY water. This shed is going to be

SO clean and *SPARKLING* ☺

(eventually).

Using the sponges to draw bubbly pictures is a LOT more **FUN** than tidying up my bedroom.

Doodling <u>and</u> earning extra pocket money is a great way to spend my time!

I'm thinking about all the things I'll be able to draw with the **ART BOX** of my dreams.

As I stand back to ADMIRE my bubble ART ALIEN, bubble Rooster and bubble Mr Fullerman, I hear a familiar voice from behind the fence that gives me a bit of a **SHOCK!**

Bubble alien

Bubble Rooster

Bubble Mr Fullerman

"Hey, Tom! What are you doing?"

HuH?

It's June from next door. She must be visiting her dad. I haven't seen her for

AGES, not since she moved schools.

 "Hi, June! I'm cleaning the windows to make extra pocket money. What are you doing?"

I ask her.

"Watching YOU make a BIG mess!" she says.

 (I've missed June ... not.)

"It's ALL under control," I explain.

"Doesn't look like it. You've got too much soap in your water, and that bit over there needs a clean."

"It's all part of my PLAN – the MORE bubbles the better."

"It's going to take you AGES. But don't worry, I'll keep you company," June tells me.

She STAYS and points out all the things I'm doing wrong. Eventually, I say,

"Better go, I've got another JOB to do!"

Then leave with the shed still covered in bubbles.

(Annoyingly, June was right about the soap.)

"You're leaving it like THAT?" June asks me.

"YES – I need to check on my washing."
(I'm hoping she'll get bored, go inside and
stop bugging me.)

 "OK – I'll WAIT for you here then."

(Oh.) NO NEED! I could
be a while. See
you later.

"Hey, Tom, are you still in a band?"
she shouts after me.

"Yes! I'm STILL in **DOGZOMBIES**, why?"

"Have you got any better?"
she says and LAUGHs.

(June is hilarious.)

BYE, June.

The washing machine has stopped and the light is FLASHING so I know it's READY.

I grab the basket and open the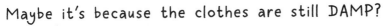
door to take everything out.
The washing feels **REALLY HEAVY**
and looks a FUNNY colour too.
Maybe it's because the clothes are still DAMP?

(I hope so.)

It's a struggle to DRAG the basket outside to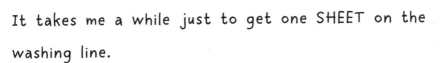
hang everything up.
Mum and Dad make
this stuff look EASY.
It takes me a while just to get one SHEET on the
washing line.
Who knew this job would be SUCH HARD WORK?

(Not me.)

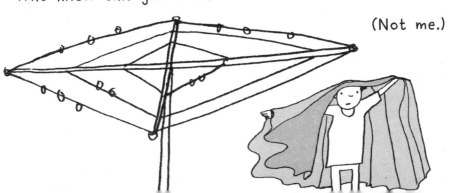

I do my best, and finally I get down to the bottom of the basket to Delia's clothes.

Or ... I think they're Delia's clothes

because they're all really ...

... small!

I hold up a tiny T-shirt and trousers.
NEVER MIND. MAYBE they'll get BIGGER again when they dry? At least the tiny clothes won't take up much room on the washing line.

(That's something!)

I hang all the (tiny) clothes out to dry, then check that June's gone before going back to the shed.

ANOTHER JOB DONE.

Getting there...

Nearly mine

No chance

Mine!

ART BOX of my dreams

All I have to do NOW is WASH the bubbles OFF the shed by turning the water back on ...

... **FULL BLAST,** which makes the hosepipe FLY AROUND like a SNAKE!

I just get it under control and aim it at the shed, when another **WASP** decides to bug me by flying around my face.

"AGH! Go away, **WASP**!" I shout.

The **WASP** takes NO notice and keeps circling round my face.

GET LOST!

AGH, STOP!

YOU'RE SO ANNOYING - GO AWAY!

I yell just as June pops her head up from behind the fence ...

... and I (accidentally) SPRAY water at her.

"STOP! What are you doing, Tom!?"

"JUNE! I'm so sorry. I was aiming at the WASP. Look! There it ~~et~~ goes," I say ...

... and SOAK her again. "Stop spraying me with water! I'm telling my dad!" June is VERY CROSS and stomps back to her house dripping wet. "I'M SORRY, JUNE!" I call out after her. Dad decides to pick this moment to come back and see how I'm getting on. (Great timing.)

BUZZ

BUZZ

The **WASP** FINALLY leaves me alone. ⸺ 🐝 BYE!
I manage to get the HOSE under control to give
the shed ONE last SPRAY of water.

"Look, Dad, I've finished!"
I tell him and point proudly to all my hard work.

Dad doesn't look that pleased.
He turns the water OFF and comes running
towards me.

Turns out I have.

I watch Dad through the now SUPER clean windows as he mops up the water from around his computer, chair, a bit on the table, some on the floor, some on the shelves and a few other places too.

He throws away some damp bits of paper that I'm SURE aren't important at all.

I wait for Dad to finish before saying, "It's a good job the lid was ON the biscuit tin. We should double-check they're not soggy, don't you think?" which makes him LAUGH.

"Yes, Tom, we probably should," he agrees and lets me choose one from the BOTTOM layer.

REsuLT!

Biscuits always cheer people up. (Job well done.)
"Do I still get my pocket money, Dad?" I check.

"Of course! After you've cut the grass with these nail scissors," he tells me.

"I'm joking, Tom."

☺ PHEW...

No ☹ chance

Getting there... ☹

Nearly mine ☺

⊙ Mine!

ART BOX of my dreams

HAPPY TO HELP
IN THE HOUSE

"What have you been doing, Tom?"
Mum wants to know.

"Washing the shed and windows to earn
my EXTRA pocket money," I say proudly.
"AND I've hung out ALL the washing too –
like you asked me to."

"I've just had a CALL from June's dad,"
Mum tells me. (Uh-oh...)
"Did you spray June with the
hosepipe and tell her to GO AWAY?"

"Sort of, YES. I can EXPLAIN."

Mum doesn't wait for me to finish.
"Oh, Tom – you should go and say sorry to June."

"It was a **WASP.**

I was trying to make it go AWAY

and leave me alone."

 "June?"

"NO - the **WASP.**

I accidentally SPRAYED her with water instead of

the **WASP.**" I tell Mum.

 "You should still say sorry, Tom."

"I DID about a million times!"

"How about you make her a card then - to

say sorry. You're good at drawing cards."

(What would Delia do in this situation?)

"I would, but I have other plans..."

I tell Mum, who gives me a "LOOK".

 "Nice try, Tom. Come on..." she says.

Mum heads outside. I *think* she's going to see
if June's in the garden – but she STOPS by the
washing line instead.

"ALL hung up nicely," I remind her.

"These have SHRUNK!" Mum says,

holding up Delia's tiny trousers.

"I don't remember putting any

of Delia's clothes in the wash, do you?"

she asks, which is awkward.

"She could wear them like shorts,"

I suggest helpfully. "And the T-shirts fit me now."

Which is a good point, I think.

"EVERYTHING'S GONE GREY too!"

Mum has spotted the sheets now.

"It's a nice shade of GREY, though, and won't

show the dirt," I add, being very positive.

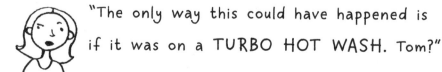

"The only way this could have happened is

if it was on a TURBO HOT WASH. Tom?"

Mum just waits for me to say something, until I have to blurt out,

"I only wanted to *SPEED* things up and be helpful."

 "I can see that. Delia will be delighted you've done her washing," Mum tells me.

"Will she?"

"NO, Tom."

(I might have to ask about pocket money later.)

tiny → T-shirt

Here are the "sorry" cards I've made.

One for June, featuring the annoying WASP, and one for Delia – so she can't get <u>too</u> angry with me.

(Fingers crossed.)

Dear June,

SORRY

for spraying you with water.

Culprit → ← Annoying wasp

SORRY DELIA

For shrinking your clothes.

(Actual size.)

HAPPY TO HELP
MAKE T-SHIRTS

Derek comes over. He's brought some old T-shirts for us to draw **DOGZOMBIES** designs on.

He spots my "SORRY" cards and says,

"Looks like you've been busy, Tom."

"I have. Just trying to be helpful, but things don't always go to plan,"

I let him know, skipping over the details.

Derek agrees, "It happens."

Then he sets up next to me at the table and brings out a drawing he wants to put on the T-shirts which looks **ACE**.

"Got any other colours to draw with?" he checks as I've only used black for the cards.

"Upstairs." I quickly go and find my BIG box of pens. There are loads more colours, but some of the lids have dropped off and the pens are all dried up.

We do our BEST by PRESSING down really **HARD,**

BUT ...

... it's a LOT OF EFFORT for not much colour.

"What we need is the ART BOX of my dreams," I tell Derek. "It's got everything we could ever want and more."

"Sounds good. How do we get one?"

"I've been trying to do EXTRA JOBS for pocket money, but it's going to take me ⇒ FOREVER to save up."

"How about we work together? Do all the jobs and share the ART BOX. What do you think?" Derek asks.

I think it's a GENIUS IDEA!

"It could be our official DOGZOMBIES ART BOX
for the whole band to use," Derek says.

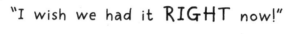

He's given up with the dried pens.

"I wish we had it RIGHT now!"

I add.

We swap back to using the nice JUICY BLACK pens
and DRAW black stars and the odd FUNNY BUG to
cover UP any STAINS on the old T-shirts (top tip).
It works a treat, and our T-shirts look GREAT!

Speaking of treats...

Two custard creams are the perfect reward for all
our hard work.

*See how to draw a T-shirt on p.249

"It's only when we pick the T-shirts UP that we both SPOT  they're not the only thing we've been drawing on.

Oh...  Whoops.

The kitchen table has a LOT of black pen marks on it.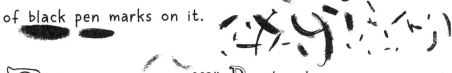

"Will they come off?" Derek asks.

"I think so. It's only a PEN."
I give the table a WIPE with a tea towel.

"I can still see ALL the pen marks," Derek tells me. So can I.
A carefully placed fruit bowl, some mugs and a few random forks cover them up — for now.

I make another quick SORRY card just in case.

Derek is impressed at my forward thinking, and we spend some time wondering what OTHER types of sorry cards we could make that might come in handy.

So many:

SORRY

I fell asleep when you were talking. zzzzzzzzzzzz

SORRY

I made a face when you sang a song. ♪ ♩

I added this.

NOT SORRY

I didn't eat the tuna sandwich.

Tuna ↓ pong

SORRY

for waking everyone up with my drums. (I will get better!)

One for Marcus.

SORRY

I found you annoying.

☺

SORRY

I was late. I blame my lack of interest.

I find Dad and let him know I'm going over to Derek's house to do more JOBS and be just as helpful as I've been at home.

"We're going to save up for the ART BOX together," Derek explains.

"So we can make more T-shirts and posters for our band," I add.

Good idea! Just try and stay FOCUSED this time, Tom ... and...

Dad says, but I am so focused on the ART BOX I don't hear everything he says...

BYE!

Rooster's pleased to see us. He's covered in DUST from rolling around in the garden.

ROOSTER!

"Mum and Dad might be outside. Let's ask them what jobs we can do," Derek manages to say as Rooster licks his face.

I check what "GARDEN JOBS" they might want us to do. Not cutting the grass "with nail scissors".

"Don't be silly, Tom – who does that?"

Errr – me?

"Let's offer to do EASY jobs," Derek suggests.

Then we practise our EXTRA KEEN faces to show Mr and Mrs Fingle how helpful we can be.

(So helpful!)

"What's brought this on then?"

Mrs Fingle asks.

They are having a tea break in the garden.

"We're trying to be HELPFUL." Derek smiles.

"For EXTRA pocket money."

 "In THAT case, let's have a think about what you could both do," Mr Fingle tells us.

 Then Mrs Fingle says "Rooster could do with a BATH" a bit too LOUDLY.

Rooster runs off.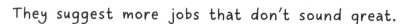

They suggest more jobs that don't sound great.

No → Cut the grass with nail scissors?

Defluff all the cushions?

Clean the mould off the bathroom wall?

Polish all the boots and shoes? * ★ *

Pair up all the old socks?

We are losing our KEEN faces FAST.
Then Mr Fingle says,
"I know! You can help CLEAN some
of my VINYL record collection."
Compared to all the other jobs, this one sounds like
it might be FUN.

WE'LL DO IT!

Derek and I shout enthusiastically.

"GREAT! Let's start
RIGHT NOW," Mr Fingle says.

"This is brilliant," I tell Derek.
"We'll be finished in no time at all."

... or maybe not.

Derek says what I'm thinking: "How many records are there, Dad?"

"Don't worry, boys – it's not my WHOLE collection. Just THOSE boxes and there's a few more over THERE."

(Oh no. This is going to take FOR EVER!)

Mr Fingle wants to show us how to clean the records properly.

So many boxes.

"Pay CLOSE attention. Hold the record like THIS and gently wipe with this special cleaner ... like this."

"Think of the ART BOX..."
I whisper to Derek.
"It'd better be good,"
he whispers back.

Once we get over the **SHOCK** of how many records there are, we TRY and get into the *SWING* of things.

I slip each record out of its sleeve – carefully.

Then hold it while Derek gently cleans the dust off.

"Keep it up, boys!"

Mr Fingle says and leaves us to it.

We SWAP over when our arms start aching.

THIS JOB IS TAKING A VERY LONG TIME!

It's hard not to get distracted by the record covers, and putting them back in the RIGHT sleeves gets tricky, but we do the best we can.

After what feels like AGES we clean ALL the records in ALL the boxes and FINALLY get the job done.

Mr Fingle comes to see how we're getting on and is VERY pleased to see we've finished.

"Well done, you two! I didn't expect you to clean ALL of the records!"

(NOW he tells us.)

"Are you ready for your special REWARD?" he asks.

"YES, WE ARE!"

we shout excitedly.

(While thinking of the ART BOX OF OUR DREAMS.)

"Close your eyes and put out your hands,"

Mr Fingle says.

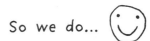

So we do...

... He gives us a packet of caramel wafers each! Normally, I'd be really **HAPPY** about this, but wafers won't help us buy the **ART BOX.**

"I KNOW how much you both love a wafer – so I thought you'd like a WHOLE packet EACH for all your hard work."

"Thanks, Mr Fingle..." I say, trying not to sound too disappointed. Derek's already eating a wafer and doesn't look disappointed at all.

"Sorry, Tom. I didn't know Dad would pay us in wafers," he tells me in between mouthfuls. "Cleaning records makes me hungry." He's right – I join in and eat a wafer as well.

"What shall we do next?"

I wonder.

"Let's go and check what's in my money box.

I'll put whatever I've SAVED towards the

ART BOX," he says, which is brilliant!

"This could really help a lot," I tell Derek as

 he takes his money box off his

shelf and gives it a "SHAKE."

"Sounds good." He smiles. There's a

promising RATTLE. I watch as he opens

it and out drops...

 A few small coins,

a tiny marble

and a KEY.

"We might need to think of something else to do,"

I tell Derek.

"At least I found my key,"

he says.

We both eat another wafer while deciding what to do next. I look out of Derek's window and SPOT Mr Akedo's car, which I can see even from here is a bit GRUBBY.

I know! We could wash cars. Look at Mr Akedo's...

That's a GREAT idea. Let's go over and ask him,

Derek suggests.

Bringing the ART BOX of our dreams just that little bit closer ...

Getting there... Nearly mine No 😟 chance 😣 😀 😊 Mine! ART BOX of my dreams

HAPPY TO WASH CARS

for the ART BOX
of my dreams

Mrs Fingle comes with us to see Mr Akedo.

"I'm VERY impressed you both have

the ⚡ENERGY⚡ to wash cars after

cleaning all those records."

The wafers helped, Mum, but we
don't want any more.

(Which is not something I EVER thought I'd hear
Derek say.)

"When Mr Akedo answers the door, let's be extra
ENTHUSIASTIC," I suggest – so we are.

"HELLO, Mr Akedo!" we say in a VERY ☆LIVELY☆

way, then get straight to the point...

HELLO!

Mr Akedo!
We wondered if you'd like to get your car washed because we'd be VERY happy to help ... for pocket money.

(It's important to add that bit in.)

"This is PERFECT timing! I'm visiting my mother tomorrow and she likes a clean car, and it's not very clean, as you can see. You could start now. What do you think?"

he asks.

"We'll DO IT!"

we say straight away.

"Wait here. I have everything you'll need,"

Mr Akedo adds.

"I'm sure they'll do a GREAT job, Mr Akedo. I'll be in the garden if you need me,"

Mrs Fingle tells him and leaves us to get started.

"If we washed every car on our street, think how FAST we'd be able to save up for the **ART BOX!**" Derek says.

"Why was Mr Akedo holding a pineapple?" I wonder.

"Who knows? As long as it's not for us."

When Mr Akedo returns, he's got TWO big yellow sponges, buckets of water, cloths, squeegees and some spray. (So much stuff!)

"You'll need to use a lot of elbow grease to get a nice SHINE on the car," he tells us.

"We can do that!" Derek says.

"Which one is the elbow grease?"
I check, looking at the different sprays.

"It's when you put a LOT of work into something, boys. THAT'S elbow grease," Mr Akedo explains.

"I knew that," Derek says.

Really?

No...

Mr Akedo tells us he'll be back with more clean water if we need it and leaves us to get on.

Derek and I get started ...

washing, wiping, cleaning, and a bit

of flicking water at each other.

"I've done more cleaning in the last day than I've EVER done," I tell Derek.

"My arms ache!" he says.

"Think of the ART BOX," I remind him.

Getting there...

Nearly mine

No chance

Mine!

ART BOX of my dreams

It takes us 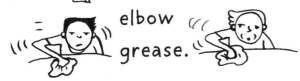 to get the car really shiny
using the ⌁ sprays and PLENTY of
elbow
grease.

When we've finished, Mr Akedo's car looks

AMAZING!

Mr Akedo is DELIGHTED with all our hard work.
(He's still holding the pineapple, which is a bit of a worry.)

"Well done, you two, the car is SO CLEAN!
All I can say is that you've BOTH really
EARNT this..."

  (Uh-oh...)

"POCKET MONEY..."

Mr Akedo finishes, then gives us two envelopes with some change inside, which is a relief. We're so pleased he didn't give us the pineapple, we forget to ask why he's got it. Mr Akedo gathers up all the car wash stuff and takes it back into his house

(along with the pineapple).

"Thanks again, boys. My mother will be super impressed with the car."

"Cleaning cars makes you tired, doesn't it?" Derek says.

"YES, and there's no way I could clean any more even if we earnt LOADS more pocket money," I tell Derek.

"I know what you mean," he agrees.

We're interrupted by Annette, who lives at number 12 on our street and is friends with my mum.

Hello, Tom and Derek. I saw you washing Mr Akedo's car and doing a BRILLIANT job!

she tells us.

Thanks!

Would you have time to come and wash my little car for pocket money as well?

"I'm not sure, Annette, we're a bit tired," I explain.

"And hungry," Derek adds.

I have snacks too if that helps.

"What kind?"

Cheese puffs and chocolate cake, if you're interested.

We let Mrs Fingle know we're going to Annette's house next, which is not far.

Luckily, Annette's car is a lot smaller than Mr Akedo's, AND she gives us  some snacks before we start, which PERKS us both up no end.

Thanks again, boys. It's so nice to have such helpful neighbours,

Annette tells us, handing over everything we need to wash her car. This time we SKIP the water flicking and just wash the car.

It's still tiring, though.

My arms ache.

My back ... aww...

We keep going until Annette's car is also clean and shiny, and we get to take home a little more pocket money to put towards ...

the ART BOX of our dreams.

"Great job, Derek," I say.

"See you later, Tom," he replies, and we do a very SLOW, slightly creaky high-five goodbye.

Aching...

Oohh...

The next morning I'm still tired because I had a **DREAM** that the **ART BOX**

SOLD OUT.

NO!

It was more like a **NIGHTMARE.**

My legs and arms are also aching still from all the car washing, which makes getting to the bathroom before Delia really hard ...

... and she beats me there.

Oh well...

Slam!

I don't mind as I haven't seen her since she realized I'd accidentally SHRUNK her clothes.

 Dad's already up and reminds me that we're going to the cousins' house today.

"Did you forget?"

"Sort of..."

"I bet Delia forgot too. Let me tell her," Dad says and knocks on the bathroom door.

GO AWAY, TOM!

is the first thing she says.

 It's Dad. Are you coming to see the cousins today?

Why not?

NO!

Someone shrank my clothes so I'm going to the market with Avril.

  I keep quiet.

Heading down to breakfast slowly, I notice there's a BROOM propped up against the kitchen door.

"Well done for washing all those cars yesterday," Dad tells me as I help myself to cereal.

"Well, I **did** OFFER to help out and do ANY JOB," I remind him.

"That's what we thought — so I've left out the broom to sweep up the leaves in the garden when you're ready."

"What? N O W ?!"

(I think of the  again.)

"Have your breakfast first," Mum adds.

The broom kind of STARES 👁👁 at me as I'm eating.

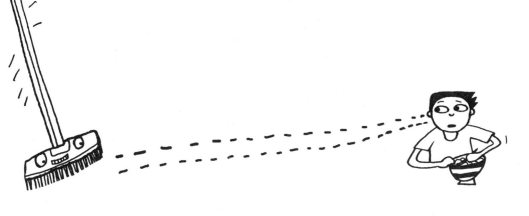

I really DO want to help out, but it's still EARLY.

So, eating my breakfast nice and s l o w l y gets me into the right MOOD for doing some sweeping.

Hopefully this won't take too long – it's not like there are LOADS of leaves in the garden.

I like this "helping out Tom", don't you?

How long will it last? Who knows?

Oh...

There are more leaves than I expected.

Seriously?

So many!

I get busy sweeping the ten million leaves that have suddenly appeared, into a nice neat pile ...

... while Mum and Dad watch through the window.
They wave and look really PROUD, which is nice. It takes a while, but it's another job DONE. ☺

HAPPY TO HELP AT THE COUSINS'

for the ART BOX of my dreams

The cousins, Aunty Alice and Uncle Kevin are all waiting for us.

"Hello, everyone. No rush," Uncle Kevin says as we arrive.

"Tom was being VERY helpful sweeping up leaves," Dad lets him know.

"He's been SO busy earning pocket money and doing all kinds of jobs," Mum adds as we go in.

"Good for you, Tom," Aunty Alice tells me.

"You COULD wash our car..." Uncle Kevin starts to say...

Huh?

"But it was professionally cleaned yesterday. You probably noticed that already," Uncle Kevin says.

"Not really..." I say and Dad LAUGHS.

"Did you hear that, boys?" Aunty Alice asks the cousins. "Tom's earning his own pocket money. I KEEP trying to get them to tidy up their BEDROOM for pocket money, but there's always an excuse why they can't do it," she tells us.
The cousins keep quiet – and so do I.

Then Mum SUDDENLY says,
"Tom can help them, can't you, Tom?"

SORRY? HANG ON A SECOND, I don't even tidy my OWN bedroom, why would I tidy up the cousins'?

Not even for POCKET MONEY.

"That's a GREAT IDEA! You missed out on cleaning our car, Tom, but NOW you can help with their bedroom!" Uncle Kevin says.

"You'd be happy to help, wouldn't you, Tom?" Dad asks while Mum smiles with that PROUD look again. And now the cousins are standing next to me like I've already said YES.

"We'll call you when lunch is ready," Aunty Alice lets me know.

"Thanks, Tom, you're the BEST," the cousins say like I don't have a choice. "It's a bit messy, though," they add.

"My bedroom's messy too," I tell them.

I can't even see the FLOOR there's so much stuff everywhere. Open boxes of games; books; clothes spilling out of the washing basket. Trainers, shoes, socks. It's like their ENTIRE wardrobe is dumped on the floor. This is going to take FOR EVER to tidy up.

"It looks worse than it really is,"
the cousins tell me.

"It looks pretty bad to me."

"Where do you want to start?" they ask.

"Where do WE want to start? We're doing this
together, right?" I remind them.

"Oh, yeah ... and we'll share our pocket
money with you, Tom," they say, which
is something.

I'm looking around at the MESS when I
SPOT a BIG pile of COMICS in the
middle of the floor. ➔

"Let's start sorting out the COMICS first,"
I suggest.

The cousins like that idea, so we clear a space and
sit on the floor.

The only trouble is, there are LOADS I haven't seen before, and we all get distracted by READING 👀 them.

(There are a lot of **COMICS!**)

I push aside their clothes and stuff and get comfy.

I get through nearly the (WHOLE) PILE when we're interrupted by Uncle Kevin shouting up the stairs,

"LUNCH IN ten minutes. CAN'T WAIT TO SEE YOUR TIDY BEDROOM!"

"We'll never get our pocket money now,"

the cousins say in a panic.

 "We could do a tiny TIDY in ten minutes," I say, and the cousins look CONFUSED.

"How do we do THAT?" they ask me.

 "I learnt this from my sister. Delia is an EXPERT at this stuff. When you're in a RUSH – like now – you do this..." I explain and start by SHOVING a load of things under the bed.

The cousins watch me and say,

 Oh, we get it now.

I do the same with the wardrobe. The cousins help me close the doors, then hide some more things under the duvets, in the washing basket and under the table too.

"We like this tiny TIDY," the cousins tell me.

We're scooping up as much as possible and hiding it anywhere we can.

The nice long curtains are an EXCELLENT place to "tidy" piles of games and books.

The cousins and I work quickly together, and before we know it ...

the bedroom looks ...

MUCH BETTER.

(From a distance.)

We finish just in time for lunch.

Aunty Alice keeps congratulating me on getting the cousins to tidy up. I take the praise and say, "It's just nice to be able to help out, especially when they share their pocket money."

"You're a good influence on them, Tom," Uncle Kevin tells me.

"It's all down to good parenting," Dad enjoys pointing out.

"AND you can tidy your OWN room now," Mum suggests.

The cousins smile and give me a look.

"We've learnt a lot from Tom. He's got very good tidying skills."

Gulp...

"When I was your age, kids, I was always doing jobs," Uncle Kevin announces to everyone.

"You cleaned Mum and Dad's car once with a metal pan scourer instead of a sponge, and left it covered in *SCRATCHES*." Dad tells him and then has a good LAUGH.

"I don't remember doing that..." says Uncle Kevin.

"I DO!" Dad chuckles.

"I think we should all go and see this tidy bedroom after lunch," Aunty Alice says.

"That's DEFINITELY something I want to see!" agrees Mum.

The cousins nudge me and whisper, "Don't worry, we've got this!"

Uh-oh...

They manage to do an EXCELLENT job of casually **BLOCKING** everyone from looking too closely at our tiny tidy.

"Right, now you've seen it, LET'S GO!" they say and CLOSE the door quickly before anyone can go IN.

(I'm impressed and relieved.)

As promised, the cousins share their pocket money with me, bringing the ART BOX of my dreams just that little bit closer.

On the drive home, Dad's trying to get music on the car radio and is fiddling with the dial.

"That was a nice lunch. Trust Kevin to not remember scratching up the car," he says with a LAUGH.

"Oh, I like this song!" I call out as some LOUD MUSIC **BLARES** out.

"Maybe not..." Dad puts on some quieter NEWS which suddenly mentions **"OAKFIELD TOWN".**

"Turn it up, Frank, we might need to hear this," Mum says, so he does.

We listen as the announcer says:

"Oakfield Town will MISS the FIERCE storm with its HIGH WINDS and RAIN that is going to cause CHAOS! A warning has been given for STORM DELIA."

"Did they just say STORM DELIA?" I need to check because this IS BIG NEWS.

 "I think they did. Sounds like it's missing our town, luckily," Dad says.

 "Why have they named a after Delia?" I want to know.

 "I can think of a few reasons..." Mum says.

"The weather people always give bad storms names," Dad explains.

 "Bad enough for the school to close?" I wonder (slightly hopefully).

 "You heard the radio, Tom, they said it won't be coming to Oakfield Town."

We pull up outside our house and I run inside to share the NEWS with Delia that she's now a FAMOUS STORM.

 Delia! You're a STORM!

She's delighted.

Brilliant, that's just what I need.

Then I pop my well-earnt pocket

money into my money box, which is filling up nicely.

The list I made for having a relaxing weekend

hasn't exactly worked out, but I've still got

the afternoon to do something **FUN**.

I make myself another T-shirt using one of Delia's

shrunken ones that fits me perfectly now. I can

wear it when I'm helping out. Only this time I put

extra paper on the table when I

use my nice black

pens to draw on it.

HELPING (in my own special way)

Top tip ------->

(I can't WAIT to have more colours to use from the **ART BOX** of my dreams.)

Looking out of a window, I can't see any sign of STORM Delia, although it is a little windy.

It's making the washing line move around a bit. Dad says it's good drying weather.

I made a SIGN to put in the window for Derek to let him know I earnt some more pocket money. He's happy about that and puts up his own sign.

I can't wait to tell Derek about STORM DELIA tomorrow when we meet up before school.

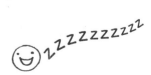

During the night, something **AMAZING** happens ...

... I have the BEST night's sleep **EVER** and I FEEL

GREAT!

... right up until I look out of the window.

What happened?

All the leaves I carefully swept up are
EVERYWHERE and now the garden looks
a TOTAL MESS.

(Almost as bad as the cousins' bedroom!)
There are broken twigs and leaves flying all over
the place, flower pots tipped over, broken plants
and the washing line's EMPTY as all the clothes
are scattered everywhere.

I get dressed *FAST* and go and see what else is going on.

Looks like **STORM** Delia didn't miss Oakfield Town after all! From the front room window, I can SEE that Mr Akedo's car is covered in broken twigs and leaves.

(All our hard work was a WASTE OF TIME!)

"AWWWWW no."

Then I SPOT something else right at the TOP of a tree, FLAPPing around in the wind like a FLAG, only ... it's not a "FLAG." It looks like a pair of pants.

(My pants.)

Oh no...

T hose pants need to come down straight away. I go and find Mum and Dad to tell them about the PANTS situation. They're in the kitchen and look a bit TIRED.

"That STORM was HORRENDOUS and so loud! All the *wind* and rain. I didn't sleep a WINK," Mum says.

"Neither did I, and it wasn't your snoring keeping me awake for a change." Dad LAUGHS; Mum doesn't. Delia comes down next. I can't tell if she's tired, but she's wearing a BRIGHT RED T-shirt (which is ODD for her).

"I slept really WELL and didn't hear a thing!" I tell everyone cheerily.

Good for you, Tom!

Delia snaps.

"**STORM** Delia wasn't supposed to hit Oakfield Town," Mum points out.

"It's unpredictable, just like the real Delia," Dad adds.

 "The *wind blew* all the washing off the line. It's gone ALL OVER the garden!" I say helpfully.

Dad makes a point of saying, "It looks like Delia has caused **CHAOS!**"

"You can say that again. There's a pair of my pants stuck right at the very top of a tree!"

Delia GROANS. "Are you going to make **STORM**  jokes all day long?"

(Probably.)

No one seems that bothered about my pants.

"Can we get them down from the tree?
They're **BLOWING** around in the *WIND!*"
I tell everyone.

"Who's going to know they're YOUR pants, Tom?"

Dad says.

"I will! They can't stay there!"
I add.

"You're right, Tom. Shall we call the FIRE BRIGADE
and tell them NOT to go to any STORM
EMERGENCIES because your PANTS need
rescuing?" Delia says like she's enjoying this.

"They're just pants, Tom. Come on, you don't
want to be late for school," Mum joins in.

"How can I concentrate in school when my pants are
up a tree? And school might not even be open,"
I say hopefully.

But Mum's not listening. Instead, she turns on the radio to hear the LATEST NEWS on the storm.

"Last night, **Storm** Delia ro**lled** in unexpectedly and brought **DISASTER** for Oakfield Town local library!

Delia RIPPED the library ROOF OFF, and RAIN POURED through all night long, **DESTROYING** many of the children's books.

BUT Great Manor School's head teacher, Mrs Mallet, has **SPRUNG** into action and has **ANNOUNCED** a **CAMPAIGN** to **RAISE** money to FIX the roof and restock all the BOOKS. The campaign will run over the next few days and other schools will be joining in. PLEASE donate and help out!

We'll have more updates throughout the day on **STORM DELIA.**

We want to hear from YOU!

Please ring and tell us if YOU'VE been affected by DELIA.

All schools are still open."

"Oh, that's TERRIBLE!" Mum says.

(I agree – I was hoping for a day off.)

I'm SAD about the library as it has the best

collection of JOLLY FRUIT BUNCH BIG books too.

  They're my favourites.

"Some schools don't even have libraries and
RELY on this one,"

Mum points out just as the radio presenter says:

"We've got a **Mr Akedo** on the line.
Can you describe the scene in your
street right now, **Mr Akedo?**"

"Did you hear that? Mr Akedo's on the
radio. Turn it up, Rita!"
Dad says.

"I hope he's OK," Mum wonders.

"There are a lot of twigs 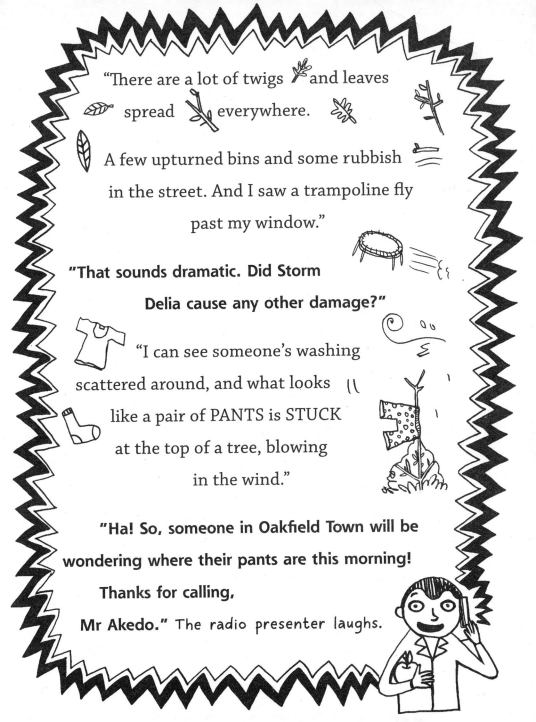 and leaves spread everywhere.

A few upturned bins and some rubbish in the street. And I saw a trampoline fly past my window."

"That sounds dramatic. Did Storm Delia cause any other damage?"

"I can see someone's washing scattered around, and what looks like a pair of PANTS is STUCK at the top of a tree, blowing in the wind."

"Ha! So, someone in Oakfield Town will be wondering where their pants are this morning! Thanks for calling, Mr Akedo." The radio presenter laughs.

Brilliant - my pants are on the radio now. That's all I need.

"Tom, your pants are FAMOUS. They've become a talking point!" Delia LAUGHS like I should be pleased about it.

 "This is EMBARRASSING." I sigh.

"Honestly, Tom, it's only local radio - no one will be listening. Everyone's got far more important things to worry about. The library roof being damaged for one thing," Dad tells me.

"Come on. Go and get ready for school! You don't want to be late. It's still windy outside,"

Mum says.

"All that time spent washing cars and sweeping leaves. It's worse than before."

I get my bag ready , then say BYE to everyone. I'll try not to think about my pants being STUCK in the tree while I'm in school.

None of my friends will have heard Mr Akedo on the radio, I'm sure.

I'll meet Derek and KEEP 👀 FOCUSED ON ...

THE ART BOX OF OUR DREAMS

At least my pants are quite HIGH UP, so no one's going to notice them.

Oh...

"LOOK, Tom, how funny is THAT?!"
Derek says when he sees me.
There's a group of kids standing under the tree,
pointing and STARING UP at my pants.

(Of course they are.)

"It must have been the **STORM** last night. It was really bad and kept me awake," he adds.

"I didn't hear it. Shall we go?"

"Don't you want a closer look?" Derek asks me.

"No, I'm good, thanks."

"Imagine if they were your pants STUCK at the top of the tree, waving and flapping around like that!" Derek LAUGHS.

 "I don't have to imagine," I whisper.

"They are your pants, aren't they?"

 "They might be. They look familiar."

Derek is sympathetic – but also thinks it's HILARIOUS.

"I won't tell anyone," he assures me.

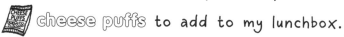
It's still *windy* as we walk to school, so I suggest we stop off at the corner shop for a packet of cheese puffs to add to my lunchbox.

As we reach the shop, we see a news sign which says:

DELIA HITS OAKFIELD TOWN: STORM DISASTER

"Why's the storm named after your sister?" Derek asks.

"It's tradition for storms to be given names. Delia's not happy about it," I tell him.

"Did you hear about the library roof falling in? Great Manor School have already started a campaign to fix it," Derek lets me know.

"**W**here did you hear that?" I ask.

"It was on the radio. **M**r **A**kedo was interviewed about it – he talked about your 🩳 pants in the tree too..."

"I was hoping no one would notice," I tell him, then open the cheese puffs as I can't wait until lunchtime.

"Do you think <u>OUR</u> school will have a campaign to raise money for the library, like Great Manor School has?" wonders **D**erek.

"We'll find out in assembly. **M**r **K**een will probably make a big announcement then," I tell him.

"Hello, Oakfield School, though I can't actually see you through my eyebrows." **D**erek does his excellent impression of **M**r **K**een.

(It's like he's actually HERE.)

 Ha! Ha!

HAPPY TO HELP
IN SCHOOL

During assembly, Mr Keen looks a little more windswept than usual. His eyebrows  are a bit **wild,** and he's got a leaf stuck in his hair.

(No one says anything.)

"Morning, Oakfield School."

"Morning, Mr Keen," we all reply.

"I hope you're all OK, and the STORM didn't cause any problems. It was very windy last night, wasn't it?" he says.

"Mr Keen!" shouts out Brad Galloway.

136

"You've got a leaf in your hair!"

"Thank you for letting me know, Brad,"
says Mr Keen as he picks it out.
I'm sitting next to Marcus, who is very quiet.
He's staring into the distance and looks sad.

  "That was FUNNY!"
I say, but he just sighs.

"I want to share the news that the town library
had its roof damaged by the storm, and lots
of books have been ruined by the rain,"
Mr Keen tells us. Everyone goes:

"AWWWWWWWWWWWWW."

 "But we're all going to help out!"
he adds, and we all cheer YEAH!

137

"Alongside Great Manor School..." he adds.

"AWWWWWWWWWWWW,"

we all groan and start muttering to each other about WHY Great Manor School has to be involved.

"We'll all be working together to help raise money to fix the roof and replace the books. Mrs Mumble is going to tell you more about the campaign later. Hands up, everyone in Oakfield School, who is

HAPPY TO HELP?"

It takes a while, but most of us put up our hands.

"We'll never get a look in if Great Manor School join in," **AMY** says, then yawns. "Sorry, the storm kept me awake," she tells me. Marcus says NOTHING.

(Which is odd – not like him at all.)

Back in class, lots of kids look tired. Julia Morton can't stop yawning.

 "All I could hear all night was the *wind* rattling my bedroom window," she says sleepily.

"The wind was so strong that it made my trampoline FLY up in the air and disappear out of my garden!" Florence tells us.

"Hey, my neighbour **Mr Akedo** saw that!" I let everyone know.

"Tom, I heard Mr Akedo on the radio – he saw some pants stuck in a tree. Did YOU see the pants, Tom?"
Solid calls out.

"Pants in a tree! That's FUNNY!"
Leroy laughs.

"How did they get there?"
Indrani asks.

"What colour are they?"
Norman wants to know.

"No idea, they're just PANTS, nothing special," I say hurriedly, trying not to make a BIG DEAL about this.

Marcus would normally be joining in and asking more annoying questions, but he doesn't say anything.

This REALLY isn't like him at all.

"Settle down, Class 5F!"

Mr Fullerman calls out. **"As you're all talking about last night's BIG STORM, while it's FRESH in your memory, I'd like you to write a STORY about it."**

Everyone starts chatting about what happened to them last night.

"Mr Fullerman, I slept through the storm, so what should I write about?"
I put up my hand to ask.

"You're good at making up stories, Tom – just use your imagination. For instance, you could write a story about how those PANTS managed to end up in that tree!"

Mr Fullerman suggests with a LAUGH.

(Maybe not.)

Marcus waves his hand. "Sir, something  **SAD** happened last night, can I write about that?" he wants to know.

 "Of course you can, Marcus. Writing down your feelings can be very helpful when something sad happens," Mr Fullerman says, and the whole class goes quiet.

Marcus stands up to say, "Thanks, sir. I want everyone to know that my cat **Tiddles** has gone missing."

(THAT's why he has been so quiet.)

 "I'm sorry to hear that, Marcus. I'm sure he'll find his way home soon," Mr Fullerman tries to make Marcus feel better.

"**Tiddles** went missing in the storm.

He was in the garden and got spooked by the wind and rain, so he ran away and hasn't come back," Marcus tells us.

AMY and I look at each other.

"I get it now..." she whispers.

"I bet he'll be back when you get home from school!" I say, although I don't have a cat and I'm only guessing. But it feels like the right thing to say.

"He might not ever come back; cats do like to wander," **AMY** says, which definitely ISN'T HELPING. I give her a nudge to stop her talking.

"It's hard to concentrate when **Tiddles** is out in the big wide world, feeling LOST and ALONE. I'm going to write a story about him," Marcus says dramatically, and picks up his pen.

(143)

Ⓗe writes ...

THE NIGHT
TIDDLES
WENT MISSING
IN THE
STORM
and hasn't been
found, so I'm really
SAD. ☺

By Marcus Meldrew

(It's a very long and sad title.)

I decide to TRY and write something to CHEER
him up. ☺

I prefer sitting next to Marcus when he's being
annoying and GOING ON about his superhero
costume.

Marcus being sad is ... sad.

MY story is called ...

TIDDLES's BIG ADVENTURE

I don't know what Tiddles looks like, so I draw his
face a bit like Marcus's:

Made-up
Tiddles

TIDDLES'S BIG ADVENTURE

Tiddles sat in the garden and moaned:

"Nothing EVER happens to me!"

Just as a big storm rolled in and swept Tiddles off the ground and UP

up into SPACE, where an alien picked him up and plonked him on his head.

into the air. Tiddles kept going right

Tiddles tried to get comfy, but his paws tickled the alien so much, he picked Tiddles up again and

BYE

meow

down to Earth, but then a BIG BIRD swooped down and grabbed Tiddles

threw him off the side of the planet, where Tiddles landed on a spaceship that was flying back flying

(148)

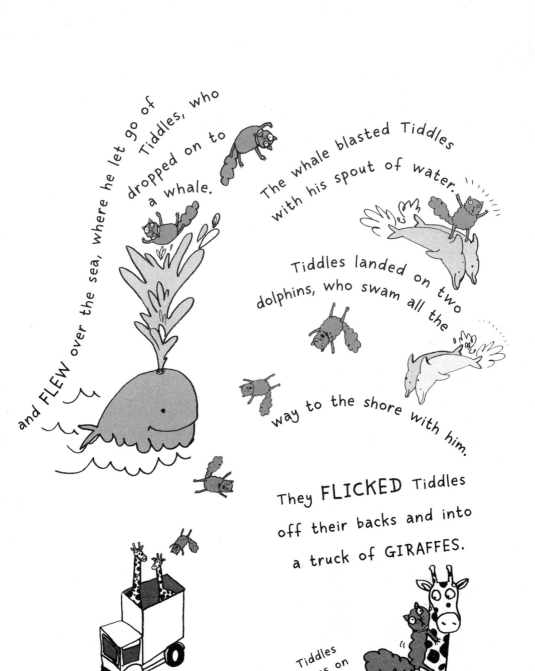

and FLEW over the sea, where he let go of Tiddles, who dropped on to a whale.

The whale blasted Tiddles with his spout of water.

Tiddles landed on two dolphins, who swam all the way to the shore with him.

They FLICKED Tiddles off their backs and into a truck of GIRAFFES.

Tiddles hangs on

One giraffe headed Tiddles like a football on to a trampoline.

He bounced UP and FLEW

(I'm going to show this to Marcus later to cheer him up.)

Mr Fullerman claps his hands to get our attention.

"Everyone listen carefully, Mrs Mumble is making an announcement."

"Morning *bswufgoweif* School. *Cbsifhowefl* URGENT FUNDRAISING campaign *djohs* for Oakfield Library *nfoieghwoiegh* help! Mrs Mallet, the head teacher of Great Manor School, *vnifhowue* has suggested that we work together *fegihgi* EMERGENCY repairs to *fix* the roof and replace the books that were ruined by the rain. There's a letter coming home with you all to explain that we're all HAPPY TO HELP! Thank you, *Oakhfhg* School!"

 As usual, Mr Fullerman has to repeat most of what Mrs Mumble says.

"Isn't it fantastic? We're <u>all</u> going to be working together to raise money for the <u>local</u> library. Two schools joining forces for a good cause. That's amazing, isn't it, Class 5F?"

(S i l e n c e.)

Mr Fullerman is a lot more excited than we are. We all know what the kids at Great Manor School are like.

Indrani puts up her hand.

"Sir, how's that going to work?"

(Good question, Indrani.)

"Both our schools will be trying to raise money in different ways. We could do a school disco, or a Bring and Buy Sale, or something else..." he explains.

"Sir, is it a competition?" AMY asks.

"No, Amy, it is not a competition,"

Mr Fullerman says.

 "That's good, sir, because Great Manor School always win at EVERYTHING."

"That's not true, Amy. We do very well at
some things..." Mr Fullerman tries to say.

 I put up my hand.

"They won the choir competition, remember, sir?"

And they beat us at football!

Brad Galloway shouts from the back of the class.

 "They got the gold medal in the design-a-flower-bed competition,"

Florence reminds Mr Fullerman.

Then Amber Tully Green stands up and says, "Great Manor School won the short story competition as well!"

Norman waves his arms around and shouts,
"They came first in the
swimming gala too!"

"It's the taking part that counts, Norman,"
Mr Fullerman points out.

Then Solid says: "Their school orchestra is
MUCH better than ours, sir."

"RIGHT, Class 5F, I want you to all know
that you are brilliant and so is OUR
SCHOOL. Let's show Great Manor School
what WE can do and raise LOTS OF MONEY!"

We all cheer at that.

"Although, it's NOT a competition,"
he adds.

"It is a competition," AMY whispers to me.

She's right about most things.

At break time Norman enjoys re-enacting the storm for us. He's very BENDY, which helps.

"We could all do a wobble-a-thon like this to raise money for the roof," he suggests.

"Though it does take a lot of effort to wobble this much!"

"How else could we raise money? We really want to do as well as Great Manor School," says AMY.

 "We could WASH CARS. That's what Derek and I have already been doing," I suggest.

"You two have ALREADY started collecting money for the library – that's GREAT!" AMY says.

 "Errr, it's not for the library, it's for the ART BOX OF OUR DREAMS."

"Oh..."

 " **"AGHHH AGHHHHHHH!"**

Brad Galloway starts SHOUTING.

"I could do a sponsored

Shout-a-thon!"

"Won't that hurt your voice?" Florence asks.

"And OUR ears..." Derek adds.

 "No, because people would be sponsoring

me NOT to shout,"

Brad points out.

(Makes sense.)

" "I could do loads of **MAGIC** tricks,"

Leroy suggests.

Then he shows us the trick he does with a

pencil. Everyone loves watching Leroy do magic.

Once he made a rubber come out of

Mr Fullerman's ear.

Even Mr Fullerman couldn't work out how he did it – NONE of us could.
We try and think of a few more A-THONS until the bell goes for the end of break.

Snack-a-thon

Sleep-a-thon

Run-a-thon

Smile-☺-thon

(There are so many A-THONS we could do.)

I notice that while we're all chatting together, Marcus hasn't joined in at all. He's VERY quiet.
As we're walking back to class, I ask:
"What do YOU think we should do, Marcus?"

He just shrugs his shoulders.

"Until Tiddles is found, I can't think of **ANYTHING** ELSE. My dad said we can offer a reward for his return, so I'm going to make **posters** to put up everywhere."

"Tiddles <u>WILL</u> come back, Marcus," I tell him.

"Sometimes," **AMY** says, "cats go and stay with other people because they like their food more."

(This might be true, but it's NOT helping.)

"Tiddles wouldn't do that."

Marcus sounds SURE about that.

"He might..."

Florence whispers.

I'm trying to change the subject when some little kids walk over to me and ask a question.

HEY, TOM!

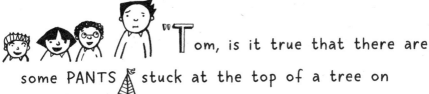 "Tom, is it true that there are some PANTS stuck at the top of a tree on your street?"

"Yes, it's true. They **won't** be there for much longer, though."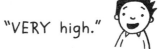

 "How high up are the pants?" one kid wants to know.

"VERY high."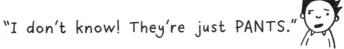

"What kind of pants are they?" another kid asks.

"I don't know! They're just PANTS."

 "I'm going to come and see them after school," the kid tells me.

"Me too - they're FAMOUS now," another one says.

"Famous for what?!" I ask.

"For being on TV!" they all say.

"Were they?" I'm surprised about that.

"Yes, there was a lady talking about the storm and she showed the pants in the tree and made a BIG DEAL about them being stuck up there. It was FUNNY."

"Do you know whose pants they are?" a kid asks me.

"No idea..." I say.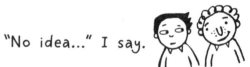

Suddenly, I notice Marcus is listening to this chat – and SMILING!

At least my pants in the tree are cheering him up a little – that's something. (I don't tell him that they're mine.)

Ha ...
Pants ...

When we get back to class Mr Fullerman is still very **cheery.**

"Did I tell you that Oakfield School have a special fundraising meter so we can keep track of how close we are to raising our target?"

"Sir, will Great Manor School have one too?" Brad shouts.

"Yes, but it won't be like ours," Mr Fullerman says.

"That's for sure..." says AMY quietly.

"I hope you've all been thinking of some exciting ways we can raise money," Mr Fullerman says.

AMY puts up her hand. "We're going to wash cars, sir!" (Which is news to me.)

There's a LOT of putting up hands!
"Sir, once Tiddles has been found, I'll join
in and wash cars too," Marcus lets us know.

 "That's good to hear – not that Tiddles hasn't been found yet, but that you'll be joining in when he is,"
Mr Fullerman tells him.

"Don't you think we should all meet up after school
and wash cars together, Tom?" AMY says to me.

"Sure – it'll be quicker in a group. It took me and
Derek ages, so the more of us the better," I agree.
(Looks like we've got a plan sorted!)
Mr Fullerman lets us have some "Golden Time" to finish
off our work or read or, in my case, do some drawing.

Marcus has already started to make his reward posters to find **Tiddles.** He is concentrating really hard and is <u>SO</u> quiet. I prefer it when he's being ANNOYING.

Looking at the pile of paper next to him, he's got a lot of posters to finish.

"Is that what **Tiddles** looks like?" I ask him.

"Yes, these posters are definitely going to help find him!" Marcus says.

(Really? I am not so sure...)

At home time, Marcus has finished all his posters and starts putting them up with some tape. He's already stuck one on the wall outside school.

"Is that **Tiddles?**" Leroy asks.

"YES, he looks just like my drawing – and I miss him." Marcus sighs.

"Tiddles looks wild," Leroy mutters.

Marcus pins up another poster.

"I hope someone finds him soon."

Then, as we begin walking home, Marcus suddenly clears his throat and calls out...

"HERE, **TIDDLES! Tiddle Tiddle Tum Tum!** Come home, **TIDDLY WIDDLY!**"

"**D**oes Tiddles answer to all those names?" I check.

 "Yes, **Tiddles** is <u>VERY</u> smart."

"But you could all call for him too," Marcus says.

So we do.

 "TIDDLESSSSS TIDDLE TUM TUM!"

"TIDDLY WIDDLY! WIDDLY TUM TUM! Tiddly Widdly Tum Tum!"

People are staring at us, but there's still no sign of **Tiddles.**

When Rooster went missing, I used sausages to tempt him back — it didn't take long,

Derek tells us.

"Does **Tiddles** like sausages?"

I ask Marcus.

"He prefers tuna."

I pull a face.  YUCK

"You're not a cat, Tom," Marcus reminds me,

then carries on shouting:

"TIDDLES! TIDDLE TUM TUM! TIDDLY WIDDLY WOO!"

While Marcus keeps searching, we all agree to meet at my house after school tomorrow to start our **Happy to Help** car washing campaign.

"I hope Tiddles gets home safely, Marcus."

"Thanks, Tom – thanks, everyone. I'll let you know if I find him," he says and then puts up another poster, before heading off home.

"TIDDLES! TIDDLES! TIDDLE TUM TUM TIDDLY WIDDLY!"

Derek and I find ourselves heading
towards the corner shop (as you do).
"I'd be really sad if Rooster went missing
                    for a long time," Derek tells me.
"I'd be sad if Rooster went missing too," I agree.
"I wonder what **Tiddles** is doing right now," Derek says.
"Maybe he's just having a rest
somewhere."
As we get nearer
to the shop we see a new sign up outside
        that says:

GREAT
MANOR
SCHOOL
HEROES
RAISE FUNDS
FOR LIBRARY

"Hey! That's not fair – what
about <u>OUR</u> school? We're
helping raise money too!" I say.
    "We should be on that
sign – how have Great
Manor managed this <u>SO</u> FAST?"
Derek wonders.
    Then it all becomes clear.

A group of Great Manor kids walk round the corner, rattling collection tins, being PERKY and POSITIVE and all looking SUPER SMART. From the sound of the tins, they have raised loads of money already.

"Hi there! We're from **Great Manor School**, and we're **HAPPY TO HELP** raise money to fix the library roof!"

Hi!

We LOVE helping out!

Happy to HELP.

Rattle

Rattle

clink

clink

clink

Any donations welcome!

"So are WE. All of us from Oakfield School. We've got plans to help too," I tell them.

"That's right – BIG plans," Derek adds.

Even the teacher who is with them looks happy – and it's after school hours. Derek and I watch as the kids wave goodbye and cheerily walk away, smiling and collecting money from people as they go.

"Our school is NEVER going to raise as much money as them, are we?"
I ask Derek.

"You never know, we might."
(We won't.)

We cheer ourselves up with a packet of cheese puffs from the shop.
We're nearly back home when Derek takes another cheese puff and nudges me.

"Look, Tom, there's a camera crew by the pants tree. Your pants are FAMOUS!"
A small crowd of kids has gathered underneath the tree.

Brilliant!

A lady is talking to the camera about Storm Delia – and my pants.

"**CONGRATULATIONS to Great Manor School** – their campaign to raise money for the damaged library roof is **AMAZING!** Here, at the **Storm Pants Tree**, these mysterious pants have become a symbol of **Storm Delia**. The people of Oakfield Town are taking pictures and asking the **BIG QUESTION:** whose pants are they? The weather today is a **LOT** less windy, so it looks like these pants will be stuck here for a while – come and see them while you can!"

As soon as the lady finishes speaking, the kids under the tree start taking photos of my pants. "This is getting out of control," says Derek.

"I know ... all this attention on just a pair of my pants!" I whisper.

"No, I meant Great Manor School taking all the glory." Derek has a point. Before anyone starts asking more questions about who the pants belong to, we head home to make our own plans.

I watch from the window as people point up at my pants, fluttering in the wind. I wish a big gust of wind would arrive and WHISK them away.

I go and find Mum and Dad to tell them that we're going to **WASh CARS** in a big **group.** They are in the kitchen and the first thing I notice is that they are both wearing

GREAT MANOR FUNDRAISING STICKERS.

★ Great Manor
★ School ★
CAMPAIGN
★

"You gave our rivals money?!" I ask.
"It was hard not to, Tom – they had a whole orchestra at the shopping centre, with their head teacher Mrs Mallet conducting it!"
"All the money raised will go to the same place, Tom – remember that," Mum tells me.

 "It's not a competition, is it, Tom?" Dad says.

"But Great Manor School always do better than our school at EVERYTHING!" I tell them.

 "I'm sure that's not true, Tom," says Dad.

 "It is kind of true," Mum points out.
Dad shows me a photo of their fundraising meter, which just proves my point.

 "It's impressive, isn't it, Tom? They really have raised a lot of money already," he says.

"We're going to have a meter too! Mr Keen told us," I say.

 "I'm sure you will, Tom."

Delia is walking past, and she can't stop herself from joining in.

"Hey, have you seen the crowds outside looking at your pants up in the tree, Tom?" she asks.

"There's a TV crew as well!"

(Yes, I have.)

"I saw them on my way in; it's no **BIG** deal," I mutter, trying not to sound bothered.

"How exciting, a TV crew. We never have TV crews round here! Let's go and have a look..."

Mum and Dad seem pleased about all of this and immediately go to the window to see what's happening. I don't want to miss out, so I follow them. We see the weather lady talking to the crowd. As we're watching, someone **WHIZZES** past...

It's only THE FOSSILS!

They fly past our house on their mobility scooter and go straight to the pants tree.

"Did you know Bob and Mavis were coming round?" Mum asks Dad.

"No – but they'll be on their way to us next. We'd better get the special jam out," says Dad.

THE LEAFY GREEN OLD FOLKS' HOME minibus pulls up and out get Vera, Cyril, Pat and **Teacup Tony**.

They join THE FOSSILS and start posing for pictures under the tree, pointing up at the pants.

Say "pants tree"!

Smile!

 "That's a cheap day out!" says Delia, watching them waving and smiling at the camera.

"I wonder how long they're going to be there for," I say.

"Looks like a while – Vera's brought a flask of tea," Mum says.

"It might not be tea..." Dad adds.

"WHY <u>have</u> my pants stuck up a tree become a thing for people to visit?" I ask everyone.

"Good question, Tom. Sometimes at the end of the news, they say 'and finally', and then tell the viewers about a light-hearted story," Mum explains.

"It's like when we all get obsessed with something and it becomes a SCHOOL CRAZE," I say.

"Exactly! Look how much your granddad is enjoying himself," Mum points out.

"Please don't let him be taking his TEETH out on TV," Delia says.

"Too late."

That's exactly what Granddad is doing.

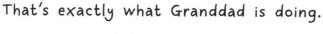

Delia sighs. "I've seen enough."

"We've all seen enough!" Mum LAUGHS.

"Come on, you lot, we've got better things to do than watch Bob do his party trick."

"I don't!" I want to stay and watch what's going on. SO many people must have seen my

pants fluttering around at the top of the tree now.

THIS thought suddenly gives me an IDEA. ←IDEA!

I could make an OAKFIELD SCHOOL

CAMPAIGN POSTER for the library roof with a

money box TIN by the tree, then people would SEE

it and might leave a donation?

Great Manor School kids haven't thought

about doing THAT (yet).

Using my nice thick black pen, I go and write my **poster**.

OFFICIAL 😊
OAKFIELD MANOR
STORM PANTS TREE

Please take a photo, then donate to the Happy to Help campaign to raise money to fix the library's roof and buy more BOOKS!
Thank you xx

I find an old money TIN to put near the tree. Mum comes to CHECK I'm not drawing on the table again.

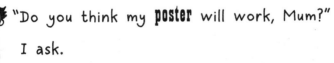

"Do you think my **poster** will work, Mum?" I ask.

"It's a GREAT IDEA, Tom, as long as no one pinches the tin. I'm sure they won't."

"Maybe Granny and Granddad will help me put it up if I'm QUICK."

"Tell Granddad not to take his teeth out again," Mum says, like he'll listen to me.

 **THE FOSSILS** are very pleased to see me.

(Some of the old folks have peaked and are sitting in the minibus ready to go home.) I don't mention that the pants are mine, but they help me set up my sign and donation box and agree that it's an EXCELLENT idea.

I notice that THEY are wearing Great Manor stickers as well.

"The Great Manor kids came to the LEAFY GREEN HOME and everybody gave them a little something," they tell me.

 "Of course they did..." I sigh.

"It's not a competition, though, Tom, is it?" Granny asks.

"No, Granny, it isn't."

(It is.)

With my sign in place and the donation box by the tree, **THE FOSSILS** start me off with a few coins, which is kind of them.

"Let's have a photo," Granddad Bob suggests, so a helpful TV person takes one for us. Might as well – everyone else is doing it. AND Granddad keeps his teeth in, which makes for a nicer picture.

HAPPY TO HELP

raise money for the library

Our school campaign has picked up a bit. There's a **BRING AND BUY SALE** planned for tomorrow, and loads of kids have already started to do their A-Thons and bring donations in. Mr Fullerman is very EXCITED to tell us about the special school meter that will TRACK ➤ how near we are getting to our TARGET.

"It will be ready in assembly, and I want you all to join in and shout 'MOVE THAT METER' really loudly to show how well we're doing."

"Let's have a practice now,"

he tells us. So we do.

"MOVE THAT METER!"

Marcus still has no news on **Tiddles** and is VERY quiet (which is sad). He's still not joining in.

"Well done, everyone. This campaign doesn't go on for long – just a few days – so we really need to do the best we can and get to the top of our meter – before Great Manor. Though it's not a competition..."

Mr Fullerman tells us.

In assembly, it's Mrs Nap that has the job of revealing the Oakfield School **CAMPAIGN METER.** It's under what looks like a big white sheet.

"This is exciting!" Norman says as he sits down next to me.

"Is it? I'm not so sure." Marcus sighs.

AMY taps me on the arm. "Don't forget we're coming to yours after school to wash cars."

"As if I'd forget that. I mean, we've got a school meter and everything," I say, looking at the white sheet.

Marcus SIGHS again even louder.
Mr Keen starts the assembly with a BIG wave.
"Thanks to everyone who brought items for the BRING AND BUY SALE. We have toys, books, MUGS, home-made cakes and plenty of fig rolls!"
"No one's going to buy those," I whisper.

"We don't have long to reach our TARGET, and Great Manor School are already out in FORCE! Although, it's not a competition. With this AMAZING METER we'll be able to WATCH our progress! Lots of you are planning your OWN fundraising, so EVERY little will HELP. Thanks to the children in classes 2P, 1H, 4R, 3S, 1F, 3A and ALL the teachers who helped make the METER. Mrs Nap is going to do the honours. Are you READY to SEE the Oakfield School METER?" Mr Keen asks.

 We all shout, "YES!"

"Wow, this meter sounds very impressive," I whisper to AMY.

Mrs Nap begins to sing.

"ARE YOU ReeAADDYY TO SEeeee THE BEST MEEeeeTER..."

She takes the sheet away to REVEAL ...

... a meter that's a bit different to Great Manor's
(that's for sure).

You can tell the kids who made it as they're the
ONLY ones who are CLAPPING.

It's made from cardboard boxes stacked on top of each other, covered in coloured paper and stuck together. There are a few balloons at the sides, and each box has a handwritten CAPTION that says:

START,

    Good going!

        Nearly there!

            and TARGET.

"Is that it?" AMY says and I agree that it's nothing special. ← Disappointed looks

Then a little kid with a cardboard ARROW on a stick POINTS to the different captions to demonstrate how it will work.

"Isn't that EXCITING?" Mr Keen asks.

                (Not really.)

"With all your fundraising, we'll be POINTING to the TARGET box VERY SOON, I'm sure. Hopefully before Great Manor – but it's not a competition," Mr Keen tells us.

                (It SO is.)

189

Back in class, Mr Fullerman SPOTS that the Great

Manor meter is on their school website, and he

looks at it on his phone.

"Let's SEE how they're doing, Class 5F,"

he says and has a sneaky look.

We can tell from his FACE that they're doing

a lot better than us.

"Nothing to worry about, Class 5F.

Just remember, it's the taking part

that counts," he tells us.

 "Sir, a group of us are washing cars, so

that will help our school get to the

TARGET, won't it?"

"How many cars can you WASH?"

Mr Fullerman asks, and he's only half joking.

"All we need to do is KEEP focused,

KEEP fundraising and KEEP moving

that meter right UP to the TARGET..."

Mr Fullerman tells us.

"WHAT ARE WE GOING TO DO?"

S i l e n c e.

(None of us can remember.)
Mr Fullerman has to remind us.

"MOVE THAT METER!
MOVE THAT METER!"

"MOVE THAT METER!"

Mr Fullerman makes us all feel VERY upbeat and
positive. Maybe we could beat Great Manor School
after all? "Finally" we might be better at something
than they are. Because when it comes to meters ...

... theirs is already pretty AMAZING.

(Although they don't have balloons...)

They're already up to TWO stars.

HAPPY TO HELP WASH CARS
for the school campaign

AMY, Derek, Leroy and Florence come round to my house after school, READY to WASH some cars with **Mr Fullerman's** encouraging words going round and round in our heads.

Norman turns up with a packet of FIG rolls.

"I got them at the **BRING AND BUY SALE,**" he tells us.

There's no sign of Marcus yet.

"Maybe Tiddles came back?" Florence says.

We all hope so. I've made some badges from sticky labels and hand them out.

Dad's coming with us and is bringing the buckets, sponges, cloths and soap. He keeps telling everyone jokes like: "What did one bucket say to another?"

"I don't know, Dad..." I sigh.

 Are you OK? You look a bit PAIL...

(No one gets it...)

Oh, Daddd...

Before we set off, Derek makes a suggestion.
"We should **ALL** smile a lot – like the Great
Manor kids do. It seems to work for them."
"Good point, Derek. Let's practise now,"
AMY agrees.

We all do our {BEST} CHEERY faces.

"People will either be thrilled to see you or
TERRIFIED." Dad LAUGHS.

There's a knock at the door, so we KEEP smiling
as Dad opens it.

It's Marcus, who doesn't look JOLLY.
"Tiddles hasn't come home yet, but I thought washing
cars might take my mind off him for a while," he tells us.

"We're HAPPY to see you, Marcus,"
I say and give him a sticker.

No sign of
Tiddles yet.

"Can we keep looking for him as we go?"
Marcus wants to know.

"Of <u>course</u> we can, Marcus. We'll all keep our
EYES peeled," Dad says.

(Which sounds painful. ☉ ☉)

"Everyone ready?" Dad asks.

"Because we've got a VERY long way to go..." *Sigh...*

Then he takes us across the road to Mr Akedo's house.

 (Very funny, Dad.)

"Hello, Mr Akedo. We're happy to help clean your car.
We're raising money for the library roof," *Agh!*
we say together.

He looks **SURPRISED** to see us all smiling at him.

"I'm so sorry, but a group of Great Manor
children have already been here and cleaned
my car," Mr Akedo tells us.

(195)

W e look at his car ...

which IS very ☆*CLEAN.*☆

"That's so annoying! Washing cars is <u>OUR</u> thing!"

"Oh, dear – I didn't realize it was a competition,"

M r A kedo adds.

"Don't worry, M r A kedo. It's <u>not</u> a

competition – is it, kids?" Dad asks us.

(It is now...)

Looking at all the other cars on our street, we now

see that every single one of them is ☆*CLEAN.*☆

"This is RIDICULOUS!" Marcus says.

(196)

Dad stays upbeat and positive.

"Come on, follow me. There are PLENTY of other streets we can try. Great Manor School can't possibly have cleaned EVERY SINGLE car!"

But as we walk around the corner, at the FEW houses with cars that need a clean, NO ONE is at home.

"What IS going ON?" I wonder.

"This isn't working out like I expected," Florence says.

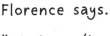"We haven't made ANY money so far," Leroy reminds us. "Not like Great Manor School."

"KEEP going, everyone. How about I tell you another joke?" Dad suggests.

This feels like a GOOD time to start calling for **Tiddles.** Marcus and EVERYONE join in.

At least we're doing something USEFUL.

"TIDDLES! Tiddly Widdly Tum Tum

Tiddly Widdly Woo!"

There's **NO** sign of Tiddles anywhere, and we're all getting a bit tired.

The Great Manor kids have been so BUSY, we still haven't found ONE car to clean.

"Right. Let's stop for a moment," Dad suggests. He's carrying all the car washing stuff, which he puts down.

Norman shouts. "MAYBE we should have done a SHOUT-A-THON like Brad Galloway SUGGESTED?"

"I've got to go home soon," Leroy tells us.

"So have I," **AMY** says.

"Me too," Florence adds.

"Dad? Where do we go next?" I check.

"**B**ack to <u>our</u> house. I don't know why I
didn't think of it before. You guys can wash
OUR car – how about that?" he asks.

"**GREAT!** Dad's got a tin of biscuits in
his shed. We can share them afterwards,"
I say, and everyone likes this idea

(apart from Dad).

"At least we'll be able to donate something to
the campaign now." **AMY** smiles.

"I'm looking forward to finally washing a car,"
Florence says.

"I'm looking forward to the biscuits."
Norman **LAUGHs**.

Tiddles!
Tiddles!
The thought of biscuits has perked

everyone up ...

... until we get back ...

... and see our CAR IS GONE!

"Where's our car, Dad?" I ask.

"That's a very good question, Tom.

Let me call Rita."

This is ridiculous,

Marcus mutters, which isn't very helpful.

Mum and Delia have gone out – with the car – and won't be back for a while.

"OK – who's good at sweeping leaves and washing windows, and I'll give you a donation for the campaign," Dad tells us.

"Don't forget the biscuits too..." I remind him.

With everybody working together, it doesn't take long to sweep a few leaves, wipe some windows and play a few games too.

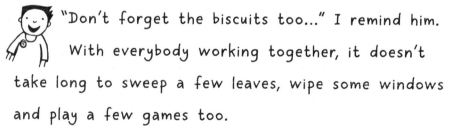

We didn't raise that much money, but we had a
lot of FUN ☺ and enjoyed
a few biscuits.

After everyone's gone home,

I ask Dad to check the Great Manor meter.

"I BET they've had LOADS of donations by

now after all those cars they washed."

"Let me check, Tom. I'm sure there's not THAT
much difference between your school and
Great Manor," Dad says, then looks at
their fancy meter on his phone.

"Oh ... wow! They have been busy. It's all for a good
cause," Dad says. "There's always your **BRING AND
BUY SALE** tomorrow. Your school will catch up."

I'm not so sure.

METER UPDATE

The Great Manor School METER looks even
more impressive when it's all LIT UP.
They're nearly at their TARGET.

HAPPY TO HELP
GET to the TARGET

At our assembly, the Oakfield School meter HOVERS around the **GOOD GOING**, though the little kid keeps moving it up and down.

$\mathbb{I}$ remembered to HAND in the money we made to $\mathbb{M}$rs $\mathbb{M}$umble. She's in charge of adding it all up. She makes an ...

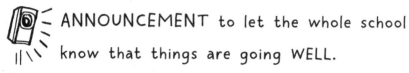 ANNOUNCEMENT to let the whole school know that things are going WELL.

(Or at least that's what we think she said.)

$\mathbb{M}$r $\mathbb{F}$ullerman CONGRATULATES all of us for HELPING out with the campaign.

"Well done, Class 5F – KEEP going. Let's MOVE that meter UP a bit further so we can BEAT Great Manor School **to the target, though it's not a competition. You're ALL AMAZING!"**

Which is nice to hear.

Then he spoils the moment by reminding us about

the SPELLING TEST. ☹

Yes! Spelling test!

The other thing that spoils the day is finding out from Marcus that **Tiddles** STILL hasn't come home

... YET.

"I really thought my **posters** would help to find him," Marcus tells us.

"I've been looking for him too, Marcus," **AMY** says.

"Me too," I add (even though I haven't).

"I did see a cat in our garden, but it wasn't **Tiddles,**" Marcus says.

NOT
Tiddles

"We'll keep looking. I'm sure he's out there somewhere," **AMY** tells Marcus.

I hope so.

(We all do.)

Derek and I are walking home together after school, and we pass one of Marcus's posters.

"Still no sign of Tiddles, then?" Derek asks.

"No," I say. **"Tiddles** looks like he's having a bad day in that poster," I tell Derek, which makes me THINK of

I remind Derek about it.

"Shall we go and look at it? I want to see how good this **ART BOX** really is!" Derek suggests.

"Yes, good idea. The shop isn't far away."

"What if they've all SOLD OUT?"

Derek says, which MAKES ME

PANIC!

"QUICK, RUN!

We need to get to the shop

because THIS is an

EMERGENCY."

When Derek sees the odd shop, he has the same reaction as I did.

"Are you SURE this is the right place?" he checks.

"You'll see... Follow me."

Derek goes STRAIGHT to the rubber SNAKE.

"Wow, how did I not know about this shop?

This SNAKE is THE BEST!"

I'm looking around for the ART BOX -

but I can't see it anywhere.

"Maybe it's been moved -

I'll ask," I tell Derek

as he's lunging at me with the snake.

I go to find the shopkeeper FAST and

ask him WHERE the ART BOX is.

Do you mean the really lovely ART BOX that was near the window?

he checks.

 "YES! That's right. That's the one!"

I say excitedly.

Those *ART BOXES* were SO popular, full of all kinds of lovely pens, paints, everything you'd need.

"I KNOW! It's the **ART BOX** of our dreams. Where are they, please?"

I'm so sorry. They were VERY popular, and we've SOLD OUT. But we do have OTHER ART BOXES,

he tells us. Derek and I are in **SHOCK.**

Huh? No!

"It's not the same thing. Are you SURE you don't have another one?" I ask.

I'm sure. But I see you like the snake. We have lots of those.

"The snake's good, but it's not the **ART BOX.**"

Derek sighs.

"Awwww — I was looking forward to using the **ART BOX,**" I say.
We don't have any money with us right now, so Derek puts the snake down, and we head home.

Shame!

 "SHAME I'll never get to see the ART BOX now." Derek is disappointed.

"What shall we spend our money on now the ART BOX has sold out?" I ask.

We walk past another NEWS poster outside the shop that says:

OAKFIELD
LIBRARY
ROOF
CAMPAIGN
NEEDS
YOUR HELP!

Derek thinks for a moment. "The RUBBER SNAKE?"

"We could," I agree. "Or we could put it towards the LIBRARY. They'll get MORE GIANT Jolly Fruit Bunch books," I point out.

"True - and IMAGINE if WE get to OUR TARGET before Great Manor!" Derek says.

"Mr Fullerman would be SO HAPPY, Mrs Nap would sing and Mr Keen's eyebrows would wobble," I tell Derek, who LAUGHS.

"Let's donate it."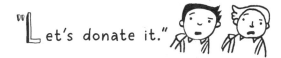

"Good thinking," I agree.

"Maybe we could keep a little to buy some cheese puffs," Derek adds.

"Let's do that. I'll take it out  of my money box tonight," I tell him.

"That snake, though." Derek sighs.

"That **ART BOX...**" I sigh.

That night I have another dream about the **ART BOX** of my dreams ... where I get one of the pens and draw a picture of a CAT.

YOWL!

The CAT YOWLS and meows a LOT.

It's pretty annoying.

Even though I'm VERY tired from all the DREAMING and SLEEP doodling, somehow, I still REMEMBER to **SHAKE** out the money from my piggy bank that Derek and I have saved and pop it in my school bag to bring to school.

I get dressed and head down to breakfast. Mum's already there and says...

"Morning, Tom. It's the BIG day today at school, isn't it?"

"Is it?" I ask.

"Don't you have a spelling test?" Mum asks.

"I hope not. But TODAY we get to see if we've got to the TOP of our meter BEFORE Great Manor School. It's pretty close. We might actually be FIRST at something for a change."

Delia comes in and says,

"That's not going to happen, is it, Tom?"

"It might."

I pick up my bag and **RATTLE** it.
"Derek and I are donating our pocket money to help the CAMPAIGN," I tell everyone.

"Tom! That's <u>SO</u> good of you. Well done," Mum says, and Dad looks very proud.

"What about your **ART BOX?**" Delia asks.

"They've **ALL** sold out. We went to LOOK at them in the shop, but they'd all GONE. The snake's still there, though," I say.

"You don't need a rubber snake, Tom," Delia tells me.   (I do.)

(It reminds me to take out some money for the cheese puffs.)

Dad turns on the radio to listen to the local news and says, "So, you're donating all your pocket money to the LIBRARY roof, Tom?"

"Yes." (Apart from the cheese puff fund.)

"WELL DONE, TOM! Every little might help you get to the TARGET before Great Manor School," Dad says.

"I hope so too!" I say. (Although it's not a competition.)

Then, on the RADIO, I hear...

And finally ...
some **GOOD NEWS!** The campaign to raise money for the library roof has gone from strength to strength...
We can **ANNOUNCE** that **GREAT MANOR SCHOOL** has reached their **TARGET** and work can now begin.
Head Librarian **Paige Turner** can't wait to restock the library with **LOTS** more exciting books. Thanks to everyone who has donated, and to the other schools that helped out too.

"**B**ad luck, Tom. At least you got a thank you as the 'other schools', though."

"It's the taking part that counts, Tom," Dad says and Mum nods.

Brilliant.

Great Manor does it again.

I'm a bit disappointed, but **M**r **F**ullerman will be GUTTED. He was really hoping we'd beat them at something.

"Oh well, it doesn't matter," I tell everyone. "It wasn't a competition, after all, and it's ALL good for the library," I say to Mum and Dad, who look all proud of me again.

(It WAS a competition.)

Morning, Class 5F!

Even though Great Manor School have already reached their **target,** we're still having a school assembly to announce how well WE'VE done.

Mr Fullerman seems in a cheery mood, which is nice. Marcus is not in a good mood because **Tiddles** is still missing. He's a bit snappy: "What's the point of doing this? Great Manor have WON," he grumbles, which actually reminds me we need to hand in our money.

"Sir, Derek and I are donating our pocket money as well," I say.

Mr Fullerman smiles and takes it. **"Thank you, Tom. Every penny counts."**

"REALLY, sir? We already know that Great Manor have beaten us to the top,"

Marcus points out.

"That doesn't stop us being PROUD of our own achievements, Marcus. We've all come together to help out, and that's what's important," Mr Fullerman says. "And it was never a competition anyway!"

"It SO was..." AMY whispers.

In assembly, Mrs Nap is playing some jolly music on the piano as Mr Keen claps and smiles at us all.

(Oh joy...)

"Well done, Oakfield School, for all the speedy fundraising you've done. Would you like to see if we've reached our target on the wonderful Oakfield Campaign Meter?" Mr Keen asks us.

We all shout, "YES!"

Someone at the back shouts NO! Mr Keen ignores them.

"Please join in and let's all say:

MOVE THAT METER!

MOVE THAT METER!"

A little kid is holding an [arrow] on a stick, and points it to the top of the meter, where it says TARGET.

At exactly the same time, Caretaker Stan strikes a GONG 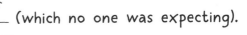 (which no one was expecting).

"I bet Great Manor School doesn't have a gong!" Mr Keen says with a smile.

 Ha!

 "I bet they do..." I whisper.

It really feels like we've done something good by raising this money – everyone is very HAPPY, ☺ apart from Marcus. Nobody knows what to do to make things better for him.

"I'm OK. It's just when I think about **Tiddles,**

I hope he's OK too." Marcus sighs.

"Maybe someone will find **Tiddles** this weekend,"

I say.

We'll see.

I hope so.

I do a drawing for Marcus with a message.

I hope your FROWN

Turns upside down SOON

Someone must know where **Tiddles**

is ... do you?

HAPPY TO RELAX
at the weekend

My list is still stuck to my wall when I wake up on Saturday. Today I'm going to focus on Number 8: Spend More Time Relaxing

(because that's what weekends are for).

Having a BIG BREAKFAST is also on my list and I'm the first person up and awake so I take my breakfast to the sofa to eat it.

I'm going to relax and catch up on all the

Jolly Fruit Bunch TV that I've missed out on. I'm just settling down when Delia comes in and SWITCHES OFF the TV!

"HEY! I was watching that!"

"Morning, Tom," Delia says breezily. "I just wanted to remind you about your donation box. I saw people putting coins in it this morning. You'd better go and check it."

"Oh, yes! I'd forgotten all about it!" I put my shoes on and head outside in my pyjamas.

$\mathbb{D}$elia comes with me because she is a nosy parker. I can see my pants right at the top of the tree still, though they look a bit **WEARY** after all the flapping about.

I open the tin  and see lots of coins inside that people have been really generous and donated. How good is this? I say.

 "You might have reached your target before Great Manor if you'd counted those!" Delia says.

"Do you really think so?"

 "No, Tom, I'm joking."

"I'll take this money to school on Monday anyway," I say - but then I hear a **FUNNY NOISE.**

"**W**as that YOU, Delia?" I ask.

"No, Tom, it wasn't."

We hear it again.

Ewwwwwwwwwwwwwwwww

"What's that noise?" Delia asks.

"Are you SURE it's not you?"

Ewwwwwwwwwwwwwwwww

Mmmeeeewwwwwwwwww

Eeeeeeewwwwwwwwwww

Ewwwwwwwwwwwww

"It's definitely not me, Tom – it's coming from the tree!"

EEEEEEMMMMMEEEWWWW

We both look up, and right at the top of the tree, right next to my pants, is ...

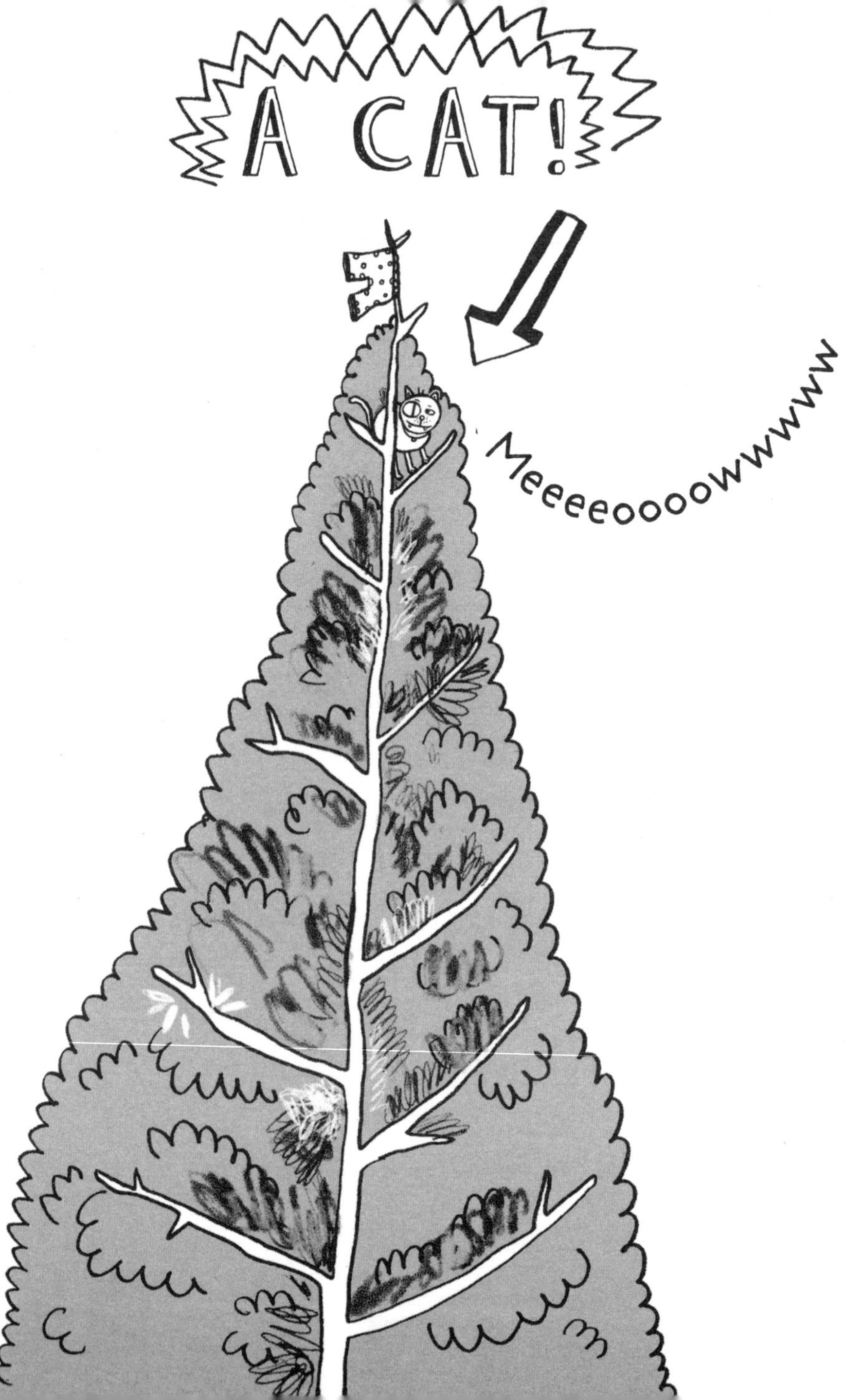
A CAT!
Meeeeoooowwwww

"It looks like a cat has got stuck," Delia says.

"It looks like it could be **Tiddles!**"
I tell her excitedly. "He's Marcus's
cat – he's been missing since the storm!"

"TIDDLES!
TIDDLY WIDDLY
TIDDLE WIDDLE
WOO
WOO!"

The cat looks down and meows.

"See! He knows his name!" I say.

"Which one?"

"All of them. He answers to ALL those names!
We have to get him down."

Delia and I try and call **Tiddles** down, but he's not budging.

"Tiddles! Tiddles! Tiddles! Tiddles!"

Tiddles is well and truly STUCK up the tree.

"We could try TUNA. He likes that." I pull a face.

So, Delia opens a tin from the kitchen, puts it on a plate and leaves it under the tree. We wait, and wait...

"That's not working," she says. (I'm not surprised, tuna's YUCK!) "I'll call the fire brigade. They'll get him down." The fire brigade know exactly where the STORM PANTS TREE is and arrive quickly.

Mr Akedo comes out of his house on his phone. He's talking to what sounds like the radio station again, telling them what's happening.

(He's still holding a pineapple.)

"It must be a slow news day in Oakfield Town," Delia says as a TV crew turns up to film the whole RESCUE.

Tiddles is brought SAFELY down to the ground along with ...

(228)

... my pants.

"Does anyone know whose cat this is?" the firefighter asks.

"Yes, it's **Tiddles,** my friend's cat," I say. Then Delia adds, "And the PANTS belong to him – my little brother. Don't they, Tom?"

"Thanks, Delia..." I say and take them back quickly. Meanwhile, the TV reporter says:

> ### HELLO!
> We're LIVE from the STORM PANTS TREE. There's an interesting-looking CAT that's been safely rescued along with the now FAMOUS pants. They look a bit windswept but have just been reunited with their owner. What a happy ending for everyone here in Oakfield Town. The weather today will be mostly FABULOUS.

We bring **Tiddles** back to our house and YES, he does look $\mathsf{EXACTLY}$ like Marcus's poster.

Purr purr

I give him some food and water, then I call Marcus and tell him the GOOD NEWS.

He's so HAPPY!

(So am I.) ☺

It's nice pretending to have a cat for a while, and Delia has to stay away (because she's allergic to pets).

Marcus can **FINALLY** take down his posters, and it's not long before the doorbell rings.

I can **GUESS** who it is.

As soon as Marcus sees **Tiddles,** he gives him a

BIG hug.

... and then he HUGS ME.

(Which is unexpected.)

"Thanks, Tom. Finding **Tiddles** is the best news EVER. I'm so happy!"

"I'm pleased that Tiddles is safe, too, Marcus!" I tell him.

Marcus's dad

"This is lovely – we're <u>SO</u> glad **Tiddles** is back with you," Mum says, and she and Dad and Marcus's dad all smile at us.

"This is for you, Tom," Marcus says and hands me an envelope. "It's a thank you card." Which is NICE of him!

"I made it myself with my fancy new pens," he adds.

"It's a **really** good card because I'm brilliant at drawing. You'll definitely like it," he says.

"I'm sure I will..." I reply.

Marcus is in a hurry to take **Tiddles** home. He'll be in a MUCH better mood at school now, I bet.

I wait until Marcus, his dad and **Tiddles** have left before I open the card.

There's a picture of **Tiddles** on the front,

Thank You, Tom

For Finding TIDDLES!

and on the inside...

Here is your
BIG REWARD!
Thank you!
LOVE MARCUS
X ♡

This is **BRILLIANT**.

Marcus has given me
the reward he promised
on the poster!

WOW

I show Delia my card and reward,
and she says, "Hey, where's MY
reward? I found **Tiddles** too."

 "HUH?"

"I'm joking, Tom. Shame the **ART BOX**

sold out. You could have got one with your reward."

 "I'll find something else – pens, cheese puffs,
maybe even that HUGE RUBBER SNAKE?"

 "Don't get that, Tom – it's annoying,"

says Delia.

(Another good reason to buy it.)

It's been a very exciting morning and I'm keen to go and relax on the sofa, finish my breakfast, watch TV and catch up with the latest Jolly Fruit Bunch programmes – there are so many!

This is EXACTLY the kind of weekend I've been hoping for. I'm just getting to a really FUNNY bit when...

Delia interrupts me AGAIN and

TuRNs IT OFF! CLICK.

WHAT NOW?

"**HEY!** I was watching that!"

"Get dressed and come with me."

"Why? I'm BUSY," I tell her quickly.

"Trust me, Tom, you'll

thank me

in the end."

I doubt that...

Delia seems like she's in a big hurry, and I don't

know why. I get dressed and follow her.

"Where are you two going?" Mum and Dad ask.

"Delia stopped me watching TV!" I tell them.

"We won't be long..."

Delia says as we head out.

"It's nice seeing them get on so well!"

I hear Dad say - which isn't really true.

"Hurry up, Tom!"

"But I just want to relax!"

Delia is halfway down the road, and I have
to RUN to catch up with her.

"Come on!"

Delia tells me. She's walking SO *fast.*

"Hurry UP, Tom, we have to be quick."

We go all the way to the ODD SHOP.

"Why are we here? Can I buy the SNAKE?"

I ask. (Obviously.)

What's going on?

NO snake.

"Don't move," she says and goes off to find the shopkeeper. I take a look around and there's no sign anywhere of the **ART BOX.** The big rubber snake is still here, so I mess around with that as it makes me LAUGH.

"Tom, put the snake DOWN and come over here,"
Delia snaps, spoiling my fun AGAIN.

I follow her through to the other part of the shop.

Where I get a BIG suRPRISE!

There's

"**W**here did THAT come from?" I ask.

Your sister called me just as someone returned this one! You're lucky,

the shopkeeper tells me.

"See - TOLD YOU that you'd thank me,"

says Delia.

"But I still don't have enough money to buy it," I point out.

"You do now - it's half price in the sale."

"I'll have to run home and get the reward money from Marcus's card!"

"Don't panic, Tom, I brought it with us," Delia says, making this the BEST DAY EVER!

The FIRST thing I do when I get home is open it up and admire the colours of all the paints and pens.

Then I make Delia a
THANK YOU CARD,
because sometimes she is actually nice and helpful (and nothing like STORM Delia at all).

HAPPY
TO HELP
open the new library!

"I've got good news, Class 5F,"
Mr Fullerman tells us. **"The library
roof is now fixed and there's**
going to be a  grand ribbon cutting
ceremony!"

We all cheer

☆ HOORAY! ☆

**"Great Manor School have been
invited too..."**

S I L E N C E.

(244)

"But sadly they have a sports day on the same date and won't be able to attend – so we'll be the only school going to the library to cut the ribbon!"

We all CHEER!

"Don't forget to bring your library cards with you."

We're excited to go to the library and get new books – and VERY excited to get an afternoon off school. DOUBLE JOY!

Marcus is also happy again – for now.

I had a SURPRISE for Derek to share
and he had a SURPRISE for ME.

← I made excellent badges

helpful bug

 (A TRUE story)

My friend Nikki came to visit with her parents, who were taking their time getting off the train. She laughed and said "I brought The Fossils", which made me laugh too.

I always remembered that and decided that in the books Tom would call his grandparents The Fossils too.

Michael Doherty
(the original lovely Fossil)

DRAW ON A T-SHIRT

Draw your design on a piece of paper. (Don't draw on the table!)

Slip the paper inside your T-shirt so you can SEE your design.

Using FABRIC pens, trace over your design. Then follow the instructions (with adult help) on the PENS to fix the design so you can wash it.

HOW TO DRAW A SNAKE

Copy the wiggly line and face shape.

Add the rest of the body and EYES.

Now draw the zigzag pattern and nostrils.

Happy to READ more BOOKS

www.thebrilliantworldoftomgates.com

Liz Pichon is one of the UK's best-loved and bestselling creators of children's books.

Her TOM GATES series has been translated into 45 languages, sold millions of copies worldwide, and has won the Roald Dahl Funny Prize, the Blue Peter Book Award for Best Story and the younger fiction category of the Waterstones Children's Book Prize.

In the eleven years since THE BRILLIANT WORLD OF TOM GATES first published, the books have inspired the nation's children to get creative, whether that's through reading, drawing, doodling, writing, making music or performing.

"I wanted to FILL the books with ALL the things I loved doing when I was a kid. It's just the best feeling ever to know children are enjoying reading the books, because I love making them. So thank you so much for choosing Tom Gates and keep reading and doodling!"

Visit Liz at www.lizpichon.com

(School photo of Liz being grump)